THE LEFT BANK

THE LEFT BANK

& OTHER STORIES *by*

JEAN RHYS

With a preface by

FORD MADOX FORD

Short Story Index Reprint Series

BOOKS FOR LIBRARIES PRESS
FREEPORT, NEW YORK

First Published 1927
Reprinted 1970

PR
6035
H96
A15
1970.

5/3/74 Eastern 8.20

CEC 5/8/04

INTERNATIONAL STANDARD BOOK NUMBER:
0-8369-3698-1

LIBRARY OF CONGRESS CATALOG CARD NUMBER:
79-134976

PRINTED IN THE UNITED STATES OF AMERICA

64608

CONTENTS

RIVE GAUCHE

THE Left Bank, for as long as I can remember, has always seemed to me to be one of the vastest regions in the world. Always. When I was a boy and lived mostly, as far as Paris was concerned, in the Quartier de l'Étoile, there were five Quarters of the world. They were Europe, Asia, Africa, the Romney Marsh — and the Left Bank. To-day, for me, the world consists of the Left Bank, Asia and Africa. The Romney Marsh is no doubt still in its place too.

In my hot youth I disliked Paris. She was stony and infested with winds; I suppose because it was mostly in the winters that I was in Paris. Stony, windy, expensive, solitary — and contemptuous; that was Paris. And I hated her.

I know next to nothing about architecture, but it has always seemed to me that it was the job of the architect, if he worked in stone, not to leave his building looking stony. A building, not a gaol or a workhouse, should look as if it were soft and warm to the touch — and that dictum wipes out all Haussmannized Paris. She

is never soft, she is never warm; she is in fact
obviously the creation of a gentleman with a
name like Haussmann working under the
patronage of an Imperial *rasta* like Napoleon
III: she is incapable of mellowing like the wines
they serve you in all the *Hotels Splendides et des
États-Unis* of the sleeping-car world; as incapable of supporting life as the refrigerated meat
that in those establishments you must eat, and,
like them, she is inhabited solely by — financiers!

I am talking, of course, of the Quartier de
l'Étoile of my youth. To-day I never go there,
or not more than a dozen times in a year, and
then only in a vehicle of sorts, going for an
evening drive in the Bois de Boulogne. But the
straight, hateful, stony streets still run out, the
Avenue Victor Hugo, the Avenue Wagram, and
all the rest of them, like the spokes of a wheel
from the Rond Point de l'Étoile. (I except from
my general malediction the Avenues of the
Champs Élysées and du Bois de Boulogne,
where I lived as a boy. They have some of the
qualities and dignities of mainroads; you go
along them to get to somewhere, even if it is
only to the Lacs of a summer evening: they are

8

so broad that from a horse-cab in the roadway you hardly note the unweathering stoninesses of the house-fronts. Certainly you have not the feeling that you are sunk deep in hideous canyons peopled by — Financiers — the feeling that broods over all the rest of that Quarter.)

One may say what one likes about Napoleon III: better men than myself have seen in him a better man than most — an idealist, a dreamer of frail dreams. But certainly when, with Hauss-mann he set to at the transmogrification of North-Western Paris his frail dream was a lasting prophecy. Not only did he find it brick and leave it machine-sawed stone, but he built a home for the worst ruling classes the world has ever seen — a home for to-day — or, perhaps, leave out the adjective. The world has seen a good many bad men, if never so many built to one pattern.

Anyhow, driving through those Avenues one does not seem to notice that they have much changed, either as to surfaces or as to populations: the financiers on the sidewalks seem leaner and less exotic, less Levantine, more American. And indeed the Levantine bucket-shop keeper has been largely replaced by the

9

Confidence Trick man of one type or the other.
The world progresses . . . but the change has
come in the view that, from one's one-horse
fiacre, one finds that one has of the Rive Gauche.
It remains geographically the same, but the
mental image has how much altered !

When I was a boy The Left Bank was a
yellow-purplish haze: to-day it is a vast, sandy
desert, like the Sahara . . . but immense. More
immense than the whole of Europe, more immense than even Australia, which, Australians
tell me is the largest continent in the world.
Why I should have these two images I hardly
know – perhaps because in my boyhood the
left bank was a distant city, and of distant cities
one sees, at night, in the sky, a yellow-purplish
glow – and perhaps again because now that I
know The Left Bank better than any other por-
tion of the surface of the globe I have realized
how minutely little one can know even of one
street thickly inhabited by human beings. Or
perhaps, still more because I should find it less
fatiguing to take the train from Paris to Con-
stantinople than, at half-past six in the evening,
when it is impossible to get a place in a bus, or
any other type of conveyance, to have to walk

from the Seine, up the rue du Bac and the Boulevard Raspail to anywhere on the Boulevard du Montparnasse. . . . I am talking of course only of half-past six when the spirits are low and vehicles unprocurable. I have as a matter of fact frequently walked quite buoyantly from the Île St. Louis to the Observatoire at a time of day when taxicabs were plenty. . . . But the impression of infinitely long walks with the legs feeling as if you dragged each step out of sands . . . remains.

And the place is upon the whole, perfection. There is here no stoniness: heaven knows what the houses are made of, but never having been cleaned or re-painted since 1792, all the houses have so rich a patina that you may well think they were originally constructed of patina alone — of the very Dust of Ages. And the streets are all so narrow and crooked that no winds have ever entered them. Not even into the rue de Quatre Vents does the breath of heaven ever enter . . . or into the rue du Cherche Midi! Austere, frugal, still, greyish: here indeed is the region of Pure Thought and of the Arts.

It is of course a region of a great many other

things — of the incomprehensible noisinesses of the Palais Bourbon as of the more massed movements of the Senate in the Palace of the Luxembourg: of the constantly growing fringe of internationalisms and of cafés more alcoholic than were the cafés of my hotter youth when one ordered a *café au lait* and mused over it for a whole evening for four sous and a sou to the waiter. Alas, to-day, in the most austere cafés of the real Latin Quarter a *café au lait* is called a *café crême* — and the crême, quite often, late of an evening, is condensed milk. It costs fifteen sous!

But the real Latin Quarter does maintain its austerities: they still, for instance, there serve you orange-flower water with your infusion of tilleul, though few students to-day know what to do with it, and still, the students of the Sorbonne in conclave and riotous are strong enough to make a government fall if they dislike a professor, or suspect infringements of their privileges. Yes, they will mob a Minister of Education sitting in the Café du Pantheon, and he will only get away under the protection of gendarmes and firemen — with the loss of his hat. . . .

Let me please dwell a little on the real Latin

Quarter, though the subject is off my line of the moment: but, in the end, the region that surrounds the Sorbonne is the living heart of the South Side — perhaps of France, perhaps still more of the world. For France has many and famous Universities, but the world has only one Latin Quarter.

It is not merely that this Quarter contains the Sorbonne, or even the Sorbonne plus the Beaux Arts: it is that these two institutions attract an infinite number of youths seriously intent on absorbing pure thought on authorized and academic lines, and, much more important still, an infinite number of youths who re-act instinctively against thought and the arts as enjoined by authorized or academic teachers. The Sorbonne and the Beaux Arts are minatory institutions in that without their warrant you cannot make any sort of official career in France or in countries where French Academic diplomas carry weight. So that, if you come into opposition with either body your chance of an official livelihood is gone: you think twice about it; your opposition is the more bitter . . . and Thought is promoted. In that way the Quartier Latin lives in a sense that can be advanced for none of our, say, Anglo-Saxon Universities which have the gift of surrounding even the most advanced of opposed thought with suavity – as you pack nitroglycerine in cocoa-butter to keep it from exploding. . . .

Around, then, this intensely living Quarter stretch infinite vastnesses of arrondissements, known and unknown. For the Left Bank is a great city in itself. Where the Boulevard du Montparnasse, running east and west, turns into the Boulevard du Pont Royal, you have a huge Quarter of hospitals, clinics, dispensaries, slums – if there can be said to be slums in Paris – the Observatory, and the great gaol. This is the XIIIth Arrondissement of which it is said that it is the largest of all in extent and the most sparsely populated, since the hospitals, clinics, Protestant Training Colleges and Institutions in general have all spacious grounds and are slowly pushing out the more densely populated slum-lands. . . .

In my hot youth – which was a pretty cool affair – all this quarter was reputed to be glamorous and filled with dangers – for it was the quarter of the Apache. Unsafe at dusk and later . . . I remember going, in the nineties, several times to visit an old artist, a friend of my grandfather's in his Paris days. He lived in the small village of studios that is next door to the Santé prison. It was enjoined on me by my careful guardians that I must never, never, find myself south of the end of the Boulevard St. Michel after dusk because of the thugs and garotters: never indeed even in the Boulevard St. Michel itself after nightfall – because of the allurements. But the old artist painted sedulously till dusk or almost, and would not much talk till afterwards, and since I came to hear him talk of my grandfather and himself in a Latin Quarter of before even the days of Murger and Schaunard and Mimi and the others – which he did very fascinatingly! – the shades were usually much more than crepuscular when, unobtrusively, I would slip out of the gates of that enclosed village. . . . A long boulevard, lined all the way with blank, high, very grim walls, darkened by plane trees then newly planted, with very dim gas lamps. Then one evening, forty yards behind my back, footsteps began to run. Until they were very close I did not even quicken my pace: when they *were* very close I ran. I ran like hell. But they gained and gained.

And they gained on me. I stood at bay under a gas lamp, beneath the walls of the prison. They emerged from the gloom – two men. They ran . . .

They were Apaches all right: there wore the casquettes with the visor right down over the eyes, the red woollen muffler floating out, the skin-tight jacket, the trousers ballooning out over the hips: and one of them had an open jack-knife. . . . I suppose they had been in an affray lower down the boulevard. The spot was just where they guillotine such inmates of the Santé as are not there for their healths. . . . For that too is one of the professions of this technical quarter. But the Apache is now extinct. He is extinct in the Avenue d'Orleans into which the Boulevard Arago prolongs itself, as in the Quarter of the Gobelins, further to the east where Industrialism which has ruined the modern world fights with the applied sciences for ground-space. For even into the otherwise nearly Utopian community of the Left Bank Industrialism must creep – and you have tanneries, producers of chemicals, of cheap footwear, of packing cases, of cheap printing – and of course of tapestry.

PREFACE

Along the Avenue d'Orleans, behind the cheap emporia, run the poor quarters, as far as, and no doubt further than, Montrouge. Here you have a population of *marchands des quatre saisons* — costermongers — market porters, odours of cabbage leaves, an Anglo-Saxon lady artist or so, a sculptor or so, window-cleaners, those who occupy themselves with graveyards because of the vicinity of the great cemetery, small — nay tiny! — shopkeepers, whose whole wares will be a peck or so of onions, five or six fish or three second-hand chairs and an ormolu mantel-clock. All in among these native dwellers push, where they can find a garret or half a garret, or a quarter, a few law students or medical students — though the student quarters are as a rule in the grim, tall eighteenth-century buildings on the high ground that supports, to the greater glory of Ste Genevieve, the Panthéon. But nowadays the students and the Anglo-Saxon lady artist or so must push in where they can and with their tiny purses and their heroically frugal lives get some shelter from the skies. So must the sculptors from every nation under the sun. And so emphatically and much more, must the midinettes, the seamstresses, the

lesser mannequins of the greater or lesser coutu-
rieres of the Other Side, and the lesser figurantes
of the theatres and all the cheerful, sensible,
careless, efficient populations of Paris that, in so
far as Paris is France, make France what she is.

For one is accustomed loosely to say that
Paris is not France: and indeed for the Paris of
the Other Side, of the Quartier de l'Étoile, of
the newspapers, of the *Hotels Splendides et des
États-Unis* or *de l'Univers et de Portugal,* of the
Financiers and the rest, the saying is true
enough, or would appear to be. You get the
sort of thing on the Côte d'Azur, at Cairo, at
Brighton, at Colombo, no doubt at Palm Beach
and very probably in Buenos Aires. But, regarded from the Rive Gauche, Paris is infinitely
more French than much of France. You get
here, concentrated, the efficiency, the industry,
the regard for the métier, the seriousness, the
frugality, and the *terre à terre,* cheerful philo-
sophy that account for the fact that only in
France can a Paris of the Other Side be a very
extended affair. As I have pointed out elsewhere, women from all over the world buy their
hats in Paris of the Other Side not merely for the
chic of the design but because the extreme care

of the seamstresses of the Rive Gauche gets an
exactness of line and ensures that that exactness
of line will be commensurate with the life of the
hat, or at any rate of the fashion. If, that is to
say, you buy a hat in London or in Frankfort or
New York, or anywhere else, except possibly
Vienna, you may possibly get something that
you can wear, but it will lose its exactness of line
after you have worn it twice. . . .

And, as with women's hats, so with thought.
The thought of France pervades the world —
because the Rive Gauche is French.

In the centre of this realm lie the Luxemburg
Gardens and the difference between the Luxemburg Gardens and Hyde Park or Central Park
New York is the difference between French and
Anglo-Saxon thought. We Anglo-Saxons believe in letting Nature alone in dreary stretches
of damp turf and the depressed trees of cities
whose air is full of coal smoke. The French are
more bold, and, facing problems more, more
exact. There is in fact no day on which a child
may not be abroad on the ordered gravel of the
Luxemburg; the days are very few in which a
child can play on the grass in Regent's Park.
The French — or the Cosmopolitan — child on

the 31st of December, between showers, can go into the walks round the fountain in front of the palace and a kindly attendant will deposit for it, a little off the middle of the walk, a little mound of sand and pebbles in which you, the child, squatting and intent, will incontinently grub with your spade and pail. There will approach you, be-caped and mournful, a Gardien – a sort of policeman. Slowly and distinctly he will pronounce to you the words Ça c'est défendu! Dé . . . fen . . . *du*! You will go on grubbing. He will repeat the words to your parent or guardian and your parent or guardian will completely ignore him. (I have done this scores of times.) The agent of the law will continue to regard you mournfully for a long interval, will then shrug his shoulders and, with sad dignity, approach another child squatting over another gravel heap. . . . Thus you will learn the lesson that Laws are made only for those who choose to keep them.

Returning to your lunch you will perceive the statues of Margaret of Anjou in plaster, of the Comic Muse, in copper, nude and on one foot, of Georges Sand, of Flaubert. You will perceive the pleached trees that run from the foot of the Medicis basin to the Odéon entrance, the very tall trimmed elms that in an admirable perspective run towards the Observatory with its austere metal domes. About these things you will ask, as successively at ten minutes to twelve each day you are conducted back home. So your earliest impression will be of serenities, austerenesses, placidities, of order, of perspective, of History, of Classic Lore, of Pure Literature; and already before you are six you will be in miniature a little man or a little woman of the French Haute Bourgeoisie, your eyes looking meditatively up the steps towards the dome of the Panthéon with its inscription in gold: *AUX GRANDS HOMMES LA PATRIE RECONNAISSANTE.* . . . And you, considering whether you shall go there in the end as Pasteur, as Renan, as Puvis de Chevannes, as Hugo — a little belated — or as, let us say, Marshal Petain! The impressions that the children living round Kensington Gardens or Central Park are other ones, so they grow up . . . well, different. And round the Luxemburg Gardens, in eighteenth-centuryish, tall grey houses, live the French Haute Bourgeoisie, austerely, frugally, coldly, with minds exact and exactingly poised, in large rooms, on Aubusson carpets, with tapestried, old, pale oak, begarlanded bergères, all set ranged for eternal Saturday afternoon conversations on serious subjects. . . . The professors, the surgeons, the doctors of law, the senators, the administrators of museums . . . the French, in fact. . . .

.But, with here and there in a nook in the great courtyards behind the houses, an Anglo-Saxon lady artist or so, or a transatlantic sculptor . . . or the atelier of a professor of painting admired by Scandinavians: these, however, in the background. . . .

That then is the Rive Gauche as far as I am here concerned. It will be observed that it contains no Financiers. And indeed, what above all marks it is a certain exiguity in matters financial, and indeed the step from the houses of the Haute Bourgeoisie round the Luxemburg Gardens, to the hand to mouth of the more distinctively Montparnassian-international regions, and to the absolute starvation of the outer fringes of those regions is but a step. The margin is the merest pie-crust, for even the professors, the surgeons, the doctors of law and the rest of the proud façade of France work for honoraria, as often as not, that an Anglo-Saxon coal-miner would despise: so do great sculptors here and painters of international fame. And if that be the lot of <u>the accepted</u> what — what in heaven's name? — is the lot of the opposition who must wait till their Thought is the accepted Thought of to-morrow? . . .

To some extent the answer will be found in Miss Rhys' book for which I have not so much been asked, as I have asked to be allowed the privilege of supplying this Preface. Setting aside for a moment the matter of her very remarkable technical gifts, I should like to call attention to her profound knowledge of the life of the Left Bank — of many of the Left Banks of the world. For something mournful — and certainly hard-up! — attaches to almost all uses of the word *left*. The left hand has not the cunning of the right: and every great city has its left bank. London has, round Bloomsbury, New York has, about Greenwich Village, so has Vienna — but Vienna is a little ruined everywhere since the glory of Austria, to the discredit of European civilization, has departed! Miss Rhys does not, I believe, know Greenwich Village, but so many of its products are to be found on the Left Bank of Paris that she may be said to know its products. And coming from the Antilles, with a terrifying insight and a terrific — an almost lurid! — passion for stating the case of the underdog, she has let her pen loose on the Left Banks of the Old World — on its gaols, its studios, its salons, its cafés, its criminals, its midinettes — with a bias of admiration for its midinettes and of sympathy for its law-breakers. It is a note, a sympathy of which we do not have too much in Occidental literature with its perennial bias towards satisfaction with things as they are. But it is a note that needs sounding — that badly needs sounding, since the real activities of the world are seldom carried much forward by the accepted, or even by the Hautes Bourgeoisies!

When I, lately, edited a periodical, Miss Rhys sent in several communications with which I was immensely struck, and of which I published as many as I could. What struck me on the technical side — which does not much interest the Anglo-Saxon reader, but which is almost the only thing that interests me — was the singular instinct for form possessed by this young lady, an instinct for form being possessed by

singularly few writers of English and by almost
no English women writers. I say 'instinct,' for
that is what it appears to me to be: these
sketches begin exactly where they should and
end exactly when their job is done. No doubt
the almost exclusive reading of French writers
of a recent, but not the most recent, date has
helped. For French youths of to-day, rejecting
with violence and in a mystified state of soul, all
that was French of yesterday, has rejected neat-
ness of form as it eschews the austere or the
benignant agnosticisms of Anatole France, of
Renan and of all the High Bourgeoisie that
eleven years ago to-day stood exclusively for
France. The youth of France to-day is con-
structive, uncertain, rule of thumb, believing,
passionate, and, aware that it works in a mist,
it is determined violently not to be coldly
critical, or critical at all.

Amongst the things that French youth re-
jects more violently than others is the descrip-
tive passage, the getting of what, in my hot
youth, used to be called an atmosphere. I tried
— for I am for ever meddling with the young! —
very hard to induce the author of the *Left Bank*
to introduce some sort of topography of that

region, bit by bit, into her sketches — in the
cunning way in which it would have been done
by Flaubert or Maupassant, or by Mr. Conrad
'getting in' the East in innumerable short
stories from *Almayer* to the *Rescue*. . . . But
would she do it? No! With cold deliberation,
once her attention was called to the matter, she
eliminated even such two or three words of des-
criptive matter as had crept into her work. Her
business was with passion, hardship, emotions:
the locality in which these things are endured is
immaterial. So she hands you the Antilles with
its sea and sky — 'the loveliest, deepest sea in the
world — the Caribbean!' — the effect of landscape on the emotions and passions of a child
being so penetrative, but lets Montparnasse, or
London, or Vienna go. She is probably right.
Something human should, indeed, be dearer to
one than all the topographies of the world. . . .

But I, knowing for my sins, the book market,
imagined the reader saying: 'Where did all this
take place? What sort of places are these?' So I
have butted in.

One likes, in short, to be connected with
something good, and Miss Rhys' work seems to
me to be so very good, so vivid, so extraordi-

narily distinguished by the rendering of passion, and so true, that I wish to be connected with it. I hope I shall bring her a few readers and so when — hundreds of years hence! — her ashes are translated to the Panthéon, in the voluminous pall, the cords of which are held by the most prominent of the Haute Bourgeoisie of France, a grain or so of my scattered and forgotten dust may go in too, in the folds.

F. M. F.

ILLUSION

MISS BRUCE was quite an old inhabitant of the Quarter. For seven years she had lived there, in a little studio up five flights of stairs. She had painted portraits, exhibited occasionally at the Salon. She had even sold a picture sometimes – a remarkable achievement for Montparnasse, but possible, for I believe she was just clever enough and not too clever, though I am no judge of these matters.

She was a tall, thin woman, with large bones and hands and feet. One thought of her as a shining example of what character and training – British character and training – can do. After seven years in Paris she appeared utterly untouched, utterly unaffected, by anything hectic, slightly exotic or unwholesome. Going on all the time all round her were the cult of beauty and the worship of physical love: she just looked at her surroundings in her healthy, sensible way, and then dismissed them from her thoughts . . . rather like some sturdy rock with impotent blue waves washing round it.

When pretty women passed her in the streets or sat near her in restaurants — La Femme, exquisitely perfumed and painted, feline, loved — she would look appraisingly with the artist's eye, and make a suitably critical remark. She exhibited no tinge of curiosity or envy. As for the others, the *petites femmes*, anxiously consulting the mirrors of their bags, anxiously and searchingly looking round with darkened eyelids: 'Those unfortunate people!' would say Miss Bruce. Not in a hard way, but broadmindedly, breezily: indeed with a thoroughly gentlemanly intonation. . . . These unfortunate little people!

She always wore a neat serge dress in the summer and a neat tweed costume in the winter, brown shoes with low heels and cotton stockings. When she was going to parties she put on a black gown of crêpe de chine, just well enough cut, not extravagantly pretty.

In fact Miss Bruce was an exceedingly nice woman.

She powdered her nose as a concession to Paris; the rest of her face shone, beautifully washed, in the sunlight or the electric light as

30

the case might be, with here and there a few
rather lovable freckles.

She had, of course, like most of the English
and American artists in Paris, a private income
– a respectably large one, I believe. She knew
most people and was intimate with nobody. We
had been dining and lunching together, now
and then, for two years, yet I only knew the
outside of Miss Bruce – the cool, sensible, tidy
English outside.

*

Well, we had an appointment on a hot, sunny
afternoon, and I arrived to see her about three
o'clock. I was met by a very perturbed concierge.

Mademoiselle had been in bed just one day,
and, suddenly, last night about eight o'clock the
pain had become terrible. The *femme de ménage*,
'Mame' Pichon who had stayed all day and she,
the concierge, had consulted anxiously, had
fetched a doctor and, at his recommendation,
had had her conveyed to the English Hospital
in an ambulance.

'She took nothing with her,' said the *femme de
ménage*, a thin and voluble woman. 'Nothing at
all, pauvre Mademoiselle.' If Madame – that

was me — would give herself the trouble to come up to the studio, here were the keys. I followed Mme. Pichon up the stairs. I must go at once to Miss Bruce and take her some things. She must at least have nightgowns and a comb and brush.

'The keys of the wardrobe of Mademoiselle,' said Mme. Pichon insinuatingly, and with rather a queer sidelong look at me, 'are in this small drawer. Ah, les voila!'

I thanked her with a dismissing manner. Mme. Pichon was not a favourite of mine, and with firmness I watched her walk slowly to the door, try to start a conversation, and then, very reluctantly, disappear. Then I turned to the wardrobe — a big, square, solid piece of old, dark furniture, suited for the square and solid coats and skirts of Miss Bruce. Indeed, most of her furniture was big and square. Some strain in her made her value solidity and worth more than grace or fantasies. It was difficult to turn the large key, but I managed it at last.

'Good Lord!' I remarked out loud. Then, being very much surprised I sat down on a chair and said: 'Well, what a funny girl!'

For Miss Bruce's wardrobe when one opened it was a glow of colour, a riot of soft silks . . . a . . . everything that one did not expect.

In the middle, hanging in the place of honour, was an evening dress of a very beautiful shade of old gold: near it another of flame colour: of two black dresses the one was touched with silver, the other with a jaunty embroidery of emerald and blue: there were – a black and white check with a jaunty belt, a flowered crêpe de chine, positively flowered! – then a carnival costume complete with mask, then a huddle, a positive huddle of all colours, of all stuffs.

For one instant I thought of kleptomania, and dismissed the idea. Dresses for models, then? Absurd! Who would spend thousands of francs on dresses for models. . . . No nightgowns here, in any case.

As I looked, hesitating, I saw in the corner a box without a lid. It contained a neat little range of smaller boxes: Rouge Fascination; Rouge Mandarine; Rouge Andalouse; several powders; kohl for the eyelids and paint for the eyelashes.– an outfit for a budding Manon Lescaut. Nothing was missing: there were scents too.

I shut the door hastily. I had no business to

look or to guess. But I guessed. I knew. Whilst I opened the other half of the wardrobe and searched the shelves for nightgowns I knew it all: Miss Bruce, passing by a shop, with the perpetual hunger to be beautiful and that thirst to be loved which is the real curse of Eve, well hidden under her neat dress, more or less stifled, more or less unrecognized.

Miss Bruce had seen a dress and had suddenly thought: In that dress perhaps. . . . And, immediately afterwards: Why not? And had entered the shop, and, blushing slightly, had asked the price. That had been the first time: An accident, an impulse.

The dress must have been disappointing, yet beautiful enough, becoming enough to lure her on. Then must have begun the search for *the* dress, the perfect Dress, beautiful, beautifying, possible to be worn. And lastly, the search for illusion – a craving, almost a vice, the stolen waters and the bread eaten in secret of Miss Bruce's life.

Wonderful moment! When the new dress would arrive and would emerge smiling and graceful from its tissue paper.

'Wear me, give me life,' it would seem to say

to her, 'and I will do my damnedest for you!'
And, first, not unskilfully, for was she not a
portrait painter? Miss Bruce would put on the
powder, the rouge fascination, the rouge for the
lips, lastly the dress — and she would gaze into
the glass at a transformed self. She would sleep
that night with a warm glow at her heart! No
impossible thing, beauty and all that beauty
brings. There close at hand, to be clutched if
one dared. Somehow she never dared, next
morning.

I thankfully seized a pile of nightgowns and
sat down, rather miserably undecided. I knew
she would hate me to have seen those dresses:
Mame Pichon would tell her that I had been to
the armoire. But she must have her nightgowns. I went to lock the wardrobe doors and
felt a sudden, irrational pity for the beautiful
things inside. I imagined them, shrugging their
silken shoulders, rustling, whispering about the
anglaise who had dared to buy them in order to
condemn them to life in the dark. . . . And I
opened the door again.

The yellow dress appeared malevolent,
slouching on its hanger; the black ones were
mournful, only the little chintz frock smiled

gaily, waiting for the supple body and limbs that should breathe life into it. . . .

When I was allowed to see Miss Bruce a week afterwards I found her lying, clean, calm and sensible in the big ward — an appendicitis patient. They patched her up and two or three weeks later we dined together at our restaurant. At the coffee stage she said suddenly:

'I suppose you noticed my collection of frocks. Why should I not collect frocks? They fascinate me. The colour and all that. Exquisite sometimes!'

'Of course,' she added, carefully staring over my head at what appeared to me to be a very bad picture, 'I should never make such a fool of myself as to wear them. . . . They ought to be worn, I suppose.'

A plump, dark girl, near us, gazed into the eyes of her dark, plump escort, and lit a cigarette with the slightly affected movements of the non-smoker.

'Not bad hands and arms, that girl!' said Miss Bruce in her gentlemanly manner.

A SPIRITUALIST

'I assure you,' said the Commandant, 'that I adore women – that without a woman in my life I cannot exist.'

'But one must admit that one has deceptions. They are frankly disappointing, or else they exact so much that the day comes when, inevitably, one asks oneself: Is it worth while?'

'In any case it cracks. It always cracks.'

He fixed his monocle more firmly into his eye to look at a passing lady, with an expression like that of an amiable and cynical old fox.

'And it is my opinion, Madame, that that is the fault of the woman. All the misunderstandings, all the quarrels! It is astonishing how gentle, how easily fooled most men are. Even an old Parisian like myself, Madame. . . . I assure you that of all men the Parisians are the most sentimental. And it is astonishing how lacking in calm and balance is the most clever woman, how prone to weep at a wrong moment – in a word, how exhausting!'

'For instance: A few months ago I was

37

obliged to break with a most charming little friend whom I passionately adored. Because she exaggerated her eccentricity. One must be in the movement, even though one may regret in one's heart the more agreeable epoch that has vanished. A little eccentricity is permissible. It is indeed *chic*. Yes, it is now chic to be eccentric. But when it came to taking me to a chemist and forcing me to buy her ether, which she took at once in the restaurant where we dined: and then hanging her legs out of the taxi window in the middle of the Boulevard: you will understand that I was *gêné*: that I found that she exaggerated. In the middle of the Boulevard!'

'Most unfortunately one can count no longer on women, even Frenchwomen, to be dignified, to have a certain *tenue*. I remember the time when things were different. And more agreeable, I think.'

The Commandant gazed into the distance, and his expression became sentimental. His eyes were light blue. He even blushed.

'Once I was happy with a woman. Only once. I will tell you about it. Her name was Madeleine, and she was a little dancer whom some *sale individu* had deserted when she was without money and ill. She was the most sweet and gentle woman I have ever met. I knew her for two years, and we never quarrelled once or even argued. Never. For Madeleine gave way in everything. . . . And to think that my wife so often accused me of having a *sale caractère* . . .'

He mused for a while.

'A *sale caractère*. . . . Perhaps I have. But Madeleine was of a sweetness . . . ah, well, she died suddenly after two years. She was only twenty-eight.'

'When she died I was sad as never in my life before. The poor little one. . . . Only twenty-eight!'

''Three days after the funeral her mother, who was a very good woman, wrote to me saying that she wished to have the clothes and the effects, you understand, of her daughter. So in the afternoon I went to her little flat, Place de l'Odéon, fourth floor. I took my housekeeper with me, for a woman can be useful with her advice on these occasions.'

'I went straight into the bedroom and I began to open the cupboards and arrange her dresses. I wished to do that myself. I had the

39

tears in my eyes, I assure you, for it is sad to see
and to touch the dresses of a dead woman that
one has loved. My housekeeper, Gertrude, she
went into the kitchen to arrange the household
utensils.'

'Well, suddenly, there came from the closed
sitting-room a very loud, a terrible crash. The
floor shook.'

'Gertrude and I both called out at the same
time: What is that? And she ran to me from the
kitchen saying that the noise had come from the
salon. I said: Something has fallen down, and
I opened quickly the sitting-room door.'

'You must understand that it was a flat on the
fourth floor; all the windows of the sitting-room
were tightly shut, naturally, and the blinds were
drawn as I had left them on the day of the
funeral. The door into the hall was locked, the
other led into the bedroom where I was.'

'And, there, lying right in the middle of the
floor was a block of white marble, perhaps fifty
centimeters square.'

'Gertrude said: *Mon Dieu*, Monsieur, look at
that. How did that get there? — Her face was
pale as death. — It was not there, she said, when
we came.'

'As for me, I just looked at the thing, stupe-
fied.'

'Gertrude crossed herself and said: I am
going. Not for anything: for nothing in the
world would I stay here longer. There is something strange about this flat.'

'She ran. I – well, I did not run. I walked
out, but very quickly. You understand, I have
been a soldier for twenty-five years, and, God
knows, I had nothing to reproach myself with
with regard to the poor little one. But it shakes
the nerves – something like that.'

The Commandant lowered his voice.

'The fact was, I understood. I knew what
she meant.'

'I had promised her a beautiful, white marble
tombstone, and I had not yet ordered it. Not
because I had not thought of it. Oh, no – but
because I was too sad, too tired. But the little
one doubtless thought that I had forgotten. It
was her way of reminding me.'

I looked hard at the Commandant. His eyes
were clear and as naive as a child's: a little
dim with emotion. . . . Silence. . . . He lit a
cigarette.

'Well, to show how strange women are: I

41

recounted this to a-lady I knew, not long ago. And she laughed. Laughed! You understand. . . . *Un fou rire*. . . . And do you know what she said:

'She said: How furious that poor Madeleine must have been that she missed you!'

'Now can you imagine the droll ideas that women can have!'

FROM A FRENCH PRISON

THE old man and the little boy were the last of the queue of people waiting to show their permits and to be admitted to the *parloir* — a row of little boxes where on certain days prisoners may speak to their friends through a grating for a quarter of an hour.

The old man elbowed his way weakly, but with persistence, to the front, and when the warder shouted at him brutally to go back to his place he still advanced.

The warder yelled:

'Go back, I tell you. Don't you understand me? You are not French?' The old man shook his head. 'One sees that,' the warder said sarcastically. He gave him a push and the old man, puzzled, backed a few steps and leaned against the wall, waiting.

He had gentle, regular features, and a grey cropped moustache. He was miserably clothed, hatless, with a red scarf knotted round his neck. His eyes were clouded with a white film, the

film one sees over the eyes of those threatened
with blindness.

The little boy was very little; his arms and
legs match-like. He held tightly on to the old
man's hand and looked up at the warder with
enormous brown eyes. There were several children in the queue.

One woman had brought two – a baby in her
arms and another hanging on to her skirt. All
the crowd was silent and overawed. The women
stood with bent heads, glancing furtively at each
other, not with the antagonism usual in women,
but as if at companions.

From the foot of the staircase leading down
from the room in which they waited, ran a very
long whitewashed corridor, incredibly grim, and
dark in spite of the whitewash. Here and there
a warder sat close against the wall looking in its
shadow like a huge spider – a bloated, hairy insect born of the darkness and of the dank smell.

There were very few men waiting, and nearly
all the women were of the sort that trouble has
whipped into a becoming meekness, but two
girls near the staircase were painted and dressed
smartly in bright colours. They laughed and
talked, their eyes dark and defiant. One of them

muttered: *Sale flic, va* – as who should say: 'Let him be, you dirty cop!' when the warder had pushed the old man.

The queue looked frightened but pleased: an old woman like a rat huddled against the wall and chuckled. The warder balanced himself backwards and forwards from heel to toe, important and full of authority, like some petty god. There he was, the representative of honesty, of the law, of the stern forces of Good that punishes Evil. His forehead was low and barred by a perpetual frown, his jaw was heavy and protruding. A tall man, well set up. He looked with interest at the girl who had spoken, twirled his moustache and stuck his chest out. The queue waited patiently.

The *parloir* was like a row of telephone boxes without tops.

Along the platform overhead one saw the legs of yet another warder, marching backwards and forwards, listening to the conversations beneath him. The voices all sounded on one note – a monotonous and never-ending buzz.

The first warder looked at his watch and began to fling all the doors open with ferocious bangs. A stream of rather startled-looking

45

people poured out, their visits over. He beckoned to the queue for others to come forward and take their places. He called the dark-eyed girl who had spoken, staring hard at her as she passed, but she was busy, looking into her mirror, powdering her face, preparing for her interview.

To the opposite door of each box came a prisoner, gripping on to the bars, straining forward to see his visitor and starting at every sound. For the quarter of an hour would seem terribly short to him and always he listened for the shout of the warder to summon him away and always he feared not being on the alert to answer it.

The monotonous buzz of conversation began again. The warder on the roof sighed and then yawned; the warder outside twirled his moustache and stared at the wall. Then a fresh stream with permits came up the stairs and he tramped forward weightily to marshal them into line.

When the quarter of an hour was over the doors were flung open again.

As the dark-eyed girl passed out the warder stared hard at her and she stared back, not giving an inch, defiant and provocative. He half smiled and actually drew back to let her pass.

The old man came last, shuffling along, more bewildered than ever. At the gate of the prison all the permits must be given up, but he trailed out unheeding. The important person who was taking those documents shouted: '*Hé!* your permit!' and added: 'Monsieur,' with cynicism. The old man looked frightened, his eyes filled with tears, and when his permit was snatched from him he burst into a flood of words, waving his arms.

A woman stopped to explain to him that if he asked for it next visiting day it would be given back to him, but he did not understand.

'Allons. Allons,' said the warder at the gate authoritatively. 'Get along. Get along.'

Outside the people hurried to catch the tram back to Paris.

The two girls stepped out jauntily, with animated gestures and voices, but the old man walked sadly, his head bent, muttering to himself. By his side the little boy took tiny little, trotting steps – three to the old man's one. His little mouth drooped, his huge brown eyes stared solemnly at an incomprehensible world.

IN A CAFE

THE five musicians played every evening in the café from nine to twelve. 'Concert! The best music in the Quarter,' the placard outside announced. They sat near the door, and at every woman who came in the violinist, who was small and sentimental, would glance quickly and as it were hopefully. A comprehensive glance, running from the ankles upwards. But the pianist usually spent the intervals turning over his music morosely or sounding melancholy chords. When he played all the life seemed to leave his white indifferent face and find its home in his flying hands. The cellist was a fat, jolly, fair person who took life as it came; the remaining two were nondescripts, or perhaps merely seemed so, because they sat in the background. The five played everything from *La Belotte* upwards and onwards into the serene classic heights of Beethoven and Massenet! Competent musicians; middle-aged, staid; they went wonderfully well with the café.

It was respectably full that evening. Stout

business men drank beer and were accompanied
by neat women in neat hats; temperamental gentlemen in shabby hats drank *fines à l'eau* beside
temperamental ladies who wore turbans and
drank *menthes* of striking emerald. There were
as many foreigners as is usual. The peaceful
atmosphere of the room conduced to quiet and
philosophic conversations, the atmosphere of a
place that always had been and always would be,
the dark leather benches symbols of something
perpetual and unchanging, the waiters, who
were all old, ambling round with drinks or blot-
ters, as if they had done nothing else since the
beginnings of time and would be content so to
do till the day of Judgment. The only vivid-
nesses in the café, the only spots of unrest, were
the pictures exposed for sale, and the rows of
liqueur bottles in tiers above the counter of the
bar, traditional bottles of bright colours and dis-
turbingly graceful shapes.

Into the midst of this peace stepped suddenly
a dark-haired, stoutish gentleman in evening
dress. He announced that the Management
had engaged him to sing. He stood smiling
mechanically, waiting for silence, gracefully
poised on one foot like the flying Hermes. His

chest well out, his stomach well in, one hand raised with the thumb and middle finger meeting, he looked self-confident, eager and extraordinarily vulgar.

Silence was long in coming; when it did he cleared his throat and announced: *'Chanson: Les Grues de Paris!'* in a high tenor voice, *'Les Grues!'* The pianist began the accompaniment with its banal, moving imitation of passion.

The *grues* are the sellers of illusion of Paris the frail and sometimes pretty ladies, and Paris is sentimental and indulgent towards them. That, in the mass and theoretically of course, not always practically or to individuals. The song had three verses. The first told the pathetic story of the making of a *grue*; the second told of her virtues, her charity, her warm-heartedness, her practical sympathy; the third, of the abominable ingratitude that was her requital. The hero of the song, having married and begun to found a family passes the heroine, reduced to the uttermost misery and, turning his head aside, remarks virtuously to his wife: 'What matter, it is only a gru . . . u . . . er!'

The canaille, as the third verse points out, to

forget the numberless times on which she had ministered to his necessities!

All the women there looked into their mirrors during the progress of the song; most of them rouged their lips. The men stopped reading their newspapers, drank up their beers thirstily and looked sideways. There was a subtle change in the café, and when the song finished the applause was tumultuous.

The singer came forward with his dancing, tiptoe step to sell copies of his song. . . . '*Les Grues*. . . . *Les grues de Paris!* . . . One franc!'

He thrust the song on to the table in front of a party of Americans, and a girl with fair hair took a copy, asking him: 'Any good? How much?'

'Very nice! Very pretty!' he assured her. '*Les Grues. Les grues de Paris!* One franc!'

'Give me two,' she said with calm self-assurance.

The pianist chalked on a little black-board and hung up for all the world to see the next number of the orchestra.

'Mommer loves Popper. Popper loves Mommer. *Chanson Américaine. Demandé.*'

Peace descended again on the café.

TOUT MONTPARNASSE AND A LADY

A T ten o'clock of a Saturday evening the ordinary clients of the little Bal Musette in the rue St. Jacques — the men in caps and the hatless girls — begin to drift out one by one. Those who are inclined to linger are tactfully pressed to leave by the proprietor, a thin anxious little man with a stout placid wife. The place is now hired and reserved, for every Saturday evening the Anglo-Saxon section of Tout Montparnasse comes to dance here.

In half an hour's time the fenced-off dancing floor is filled by couples dancing with the slightly strained expressions characteristic of the Anglo-Saxon who, though wishing to enjoy himself, is not yet sufficiently primed to let himself become animated. So even the best dancers look tense and grim though they sway and glide with great skill and have the concentrated air of people engaged in some difficult but extremely important gymnastic exercise.

Most of the men are young, thin, willowy;

53

carefully picturesque and temperamental, they wear jerseys or shirts open at the neck. Most of the women are not so young, with that tendency to be thick about the ankles and incongruous about the shoes, which is nearly always to be found in the really intelligent woman.

For they are very intelligent, all these people. They paint, they write, they express themselves in innumerable ways. It is Chelsea, London, with a large dash of Greenwich Village, New York, to liven it, and a slight sprinkling of Moscow, Christiania and even of Paris to give incongruous local colourings. The musicians are in a tiny gallery, a concertina, a banjo and a violin — the concertina, a gay soul who winks and smiles violently at every woman whose eye he can catch. At the door sit watchfully two little French policemen with enormous moustaches. After each dance *tout Montparnasse* sits at the little tables in the body of the hall or stands at the pewter covered bar and drinks *fine à l'eau* — a surprisingly weak *fine*. Nevertheless, as the evening progresses they grow gayer and gayer. . . . And more outspoken. . . .

Thus one evening a very romantic lady, an

American fashion artist, who was there to be thrilled, after having read the *Trilby* of du Maurier, and the novels of Francis Carco, which tell of the lives of the apaches of to-day, expressed her candid opinion of a supposed Dope Fiend who sat in a corner, glassy eyed, his head against the wall, his face of an extreme pallor. He was as a matter of fact a very hard-working and on the whole abstemious portrait-painter, who, having been struck with an inspiration for his next picture, was merely gazing into infinity with the happy intenseness of one about to grasp a beautiful vision.

'*Why* bring people like that?' she inquired hotly. 'Why?' She went on to explain how easy it is to be broad-minded and perfectly respectable, to combine art, passion, cleanliness, efficiency and an eye to the main chance. 'But one must know where to draw the line. *That* is an instance of how not to do it!'

Sipping her third artificial lemonade she gazed with an intense reproof at the pallid gentleman. Suddenly he glared back. He was suspecting her of taking mental notes of him for journalistic purposes or perhaps, oh horror, of having designs upon his peace of mind. He

55

rose, shook himself, and thus disturbed in his musings, lamented:

'Oh God! How I hate women who write! How I *hate* them!' in an agreeable voice.

Someone now enlightened the romantic lady as to the distinction and sobriety of her late victim, and thus robbed of her thrill, over her fourth lemonade she began to yearn for the free life of the Apache and to wish that some of the original clients of the Bal Musette had stayed. . . . There had been a dark man in a red muffler, his cap well down over his eyes. . . . Or a girl in a check dress with something about the way her hair grew. And the air with which she wore her shabby frock and walked had been graceful . . . exciting. . . . Provocative! . . . The brain groped vaguely for the word. Melancholy descended upon that romantic fashion artist, and discontent with her *milieu*. In her youth she had considered herself meant for higher things! . . . Artificial lemonade of the sort supplied at the Bal Musette is greatly conducive to melancholy.

'I don't get any *kick* out of Anglo-Saxons,' she said out loud. 'They don't. . . . They *don't* . . . stimulate my imagination!'

Nobody listened to her and upon her the infinite sadness of the world descended.

At a quarter to one the music stopped and *tout Montparnasse* by this time very lively indeed ordered its last drink at the bar preparatory to drifting on elsewhere.

The romantic lady finished her sixth lemonade and then perceived her *ci-devant Dope Fiend*.

Solitary at the end of the room he sat, one long thin arm clasping his pallid head, his body drooping complicatedly over a little table top, his face expressive of the uttermost dejection, the uttermost remorse.

Inspiration came to the romantic lady. She had been told that this was a successful and respectable portrait-painter as she was a successful and respectable fashion artist. . . . He like herself must now despise his success and must mourn for the higher ideals of his youth. . . . Though he was very young!

Then . . . Here was a kindred spirit. Here was someone else who, at one o'clock in the morning at a Bal Musette in Montparnasse, saw the empty grimness of life. Saw it! Knew he would never express it – and despaired. It is

57

thus that, fortified by artificial lemonade, the romantic mind moves.

She drifted across the room, put a hand on his melancholy shoulder and murmured:

'You are sad! I am so sorry! I understand!'

The young man lifted a heavy head and blinked several times. Smiling in a vaguely happy way, for although normally abstemious, on a Saturday night he could condescend like others, he looked at the lady. Then, recognizing her, panic came into his eyes and he looked wildly round as if for help.

'I!' he exclaimed indignantly. 'I'm as happy as a sandboy!'

From a little distance a friend swooped on him, heaved him up, said in a bored and patient voice: '*Come on*, Guy!' and marched him efficiently away. From the back he looked like a helpless, lovable child being led away by its nurse. The tragic lady sighed and made ready to depart. The proprietor served a last Porto to the remaining few. The Saturday dance of Tout Montparnasse was over.

MANNEQUIN

TWELVE o'clock. Déjeuner chez Jeanne Veron, Place Vendôme.

Anna, dressed in the black cotton, chemise-like garment of the mannequin off duty was trying to find her way along dark passages and down complicated flights of stairs to the underground room where lunch was served.

She was shivering, for she had forgotten her coat, and the garment that she wore was very short, sleeveless, displaying her rose-coloured stockings to the knee. Her hair was flamingly and honestly red; her eyes, which were very gentle in expression, brown and heavily shadowed with kohl; her face small and pale under its professional rouge. She was fragile, like a delicate child, her arms pathetically thin. It was to her legs that she owed this dazzling, this incredible opportunity.

Madame Veron, white-haired with black eyes, incredibly distinguished, who had given them one sweeping glance, the glance of the connoisseur, smiled imperiously and engaged her at an exceedingly small salary. As a beginner, Madame explained, Anna could not expect more. She was to wear the *jeune fille* dresses. Another smile, another sharp glance.

Anna was conducted from the Presence by an underling who helped her to take off the frock she had worn temporarily for the interview. Aspirants for an engagement are always dressed in a model of the house.

She had spent yesterday afternoon in a delirium tempered by a feeling of exaggerated reality, and in buying the necessary make up. It had been such a forlorn hope, answering the advertisement.

The morning had been dream-like. At the back of the wonderfully decorated salons she had found an unexpected sombreness; the place, empty, would have been dingy and melancholy, countless puzzling corridors and staircases, a rabbit warren and a labyrinth. She despaired of ever finding her way.

In the mannequins' dressing-room she spent a shy hour making up her face — in an extraordinary and distinctive atmosphere of slimness and beauty; white arms and faces vivid with rouge; raucous voices and the smell of cosmetics; silken lingerie. Coldly critical glances were bestowed upon Anna's reflexion in the glass. None of them looked at her directly. . . . A depressing room, taken by itself, bare and cold, a very inadequate conservatory for these human flowers. Saleswomen in black rushed in and out, talking in sharp voices; a very old woman hovered, helpful and shapeless, showing Anna where to hang her clothes, presenting to her the black garment that Anna was wearing, going to lunch. She smiled with professional motherliness, her little, sharp, black eyes travelling rapidly from *la nouvelle's* hair to her ankles and back again.

She was Madame Pecard, the dresser.

Before Anna had spoken a word she was called away by a small boy in buttons to her destination in one of the salons: there, under the eye of a *vendeuse*, she had to learn the way to wear the innocent and springlike air and garb of the *jeune fille*. Behind a yellow, silken screen she was hustled into a leather coat and paraded under the cold eyes of an American buyer. . . . This was the week when the spring models are shown to important people from big shops of all over Europe and America: the most critical

week of the season. . . . The American buyer
said that he would have that, but with an inch on
to the collar and larger cuffs. In vain the saleswoman, in her best English with its odd Chi-
cago accent, protested that that would completely ruin the *chic* of the model. The American buyer knew what he wanted and saw that he
got it.

The *vendeuse* sighed, but there was a note of
admiration in her voice. She respected Americans: they were not like the English, who, under
a surface of annoying moroseness of manner,
were notoriously timid and easy to turn round
your finger.

'Was that all right?' Behind the screen one
of the saleswomen smiled encouragingly and
nodded. The other shrugged her shoulders.
She had small, close-set eyes, a long thin nose
and tight lips of the regulation puce colour.
Behind her silken screen Anna sat on a high
white stool. She felt that she appeared charming and troubled. The white and gold of the
salon suited her red hair.

A short morning. For the mannequin's day
begins at ten and the process of making up lasts
an hour. The friendly saleswoman volunteered

the information that her name was Jeannine,
that she was in the lingerie, that she considered
Anna *rudement jolie*, that noon was Anna's lunch
hour. She must go down the corridor and up
those stairs, through the big salon then. . . .
Anyone would tell her. But Anna, lost in the
labyrinth, was too shy to ask her way. Besides,
she was not sorry to have time to brace herself
for the ordeal. She had reached the regions of
utility and oilcloth: the decorative salons were
far overhead. . . . Then the smell of food —
almost visible, it was so cloud-like and
heavy, came to her nostrils, and high-noted,
and sibilant, a buzz of conversation made
her draw a deep breath. She pushed a door
open.

She was in a big, very low-ceilinged room, all
the floor space occupied by long wooden tables
with no cloths. . . . She was sitting at the
mannequins' table, gazing at a thick and hideous white china plate, a twisted tin fork, a
wooden-handled stained knife, a tumbler so
thick it seemed unbreakable.

There were twelve mannequins at Jeanne
Veron's: six of them were lunching, the others
still paraded, goddess like, till their turn came

for rest and refreshment. Each of the twelve was of a distinct and separate type: each of the twelve knew her type and kept to it, practising rigidly in clothing, manner, voice and conversation.

Round the austere table were now seated: Babette, the *gamine*, the traditional *blonde enfant:* Mona, tall and darkly beautiful, the *femme fatale*, the wearer of sumptuous evening gowns. Georgette was the *garçonne*: Simone with green eyes Anna knew instantly for a cat whom men would and did adore, a sleek, white, purring, long-lashed creature. . . . Eliane was the star of the collection.

Eliane was frankly ugly and it did not matter: no doubt Lilith, from whom she was obviously descended, had been ugly too. Her hair was henna-tinted, her eyes small and black, her complexion bad under her thick make-up. Her hips were extraordinarily slim, her hands and feet exquisite, every movement she made was as graceful as a flower's in the wind. Her walk . . . But it was her walk which made her there the star and earned her a salary quite fabulous for Madame Veron's, where large salaries were not the rule. . . . Her walk and her 'chic of the devil' which lit an expression of admiration in even the cold eyes of American buyers.

Liliane was a quiet girl, pleasant-mannered. She wore a ring with a beautiful emerald on one long, slim finger, and in her small eyes were both intelligence and mystery.

Madame Pecard, the dresser, was seated at the head of the mannequin's table, talking loudly, unlistened to, and gazing benevolently at her flock.

At other tables sat the sewing girls, pale-faced, black-frocked – the workers, heroically gay, but with the stamp of labour on them: and the saleswomen. The mannequins, with their sensual, blatant charms and their painted faces were watched covertly and envied and apart.

Babette the *blonde enfant* was next to Anna, and having started the conversation with a few good, round oaths at the quality of the sardines, announced proudly that she could speak English and knew London very well. She began to tell Anna the history of her adventures in the city of coldness, dark and fogs. . . . She had gone to a job as a mannequin in Bond Street and the villainous proprietor of the shop having tried to make love to her and she being rigidly virtuous, she had left. And another job, Anna must figure to herself, had been impossible to get, for she, Babette, was too small and slim for the Anglo-Saxon idea of a mannequin.

She stopped to shout in a loud voice to the woman who was serving: 'Hé, my old one, don't forget your little Babette. . . .'

Opposite, Simone the cat and the sportive Georgette were having a low-voiced conversation about the triste-ness of a monsieur of their acquaintance. 'I said to him,' Georgette finished decisively, 'Nothing to be done, my rabbit. You have not well looked at me, little one. In my place would you not have done the same?'

She broke off when she realized that the others were listening, and smiled in a friendly way at Anna.

She too, it appeared, had ambitions to go to London because the salaries were so much better there. Was it difficult? Did they really like French girls? Parisiennes?

The conversation became general.

'The English boys are nice,' said Babette, winking one divinely candid eye. 'I had a chic type who used to take me to dinner at the Empire Palace. Oh, a pretty boy. . . .'

'It is the most chic restaurant in London,' she added importantly.

The meal reached the stage of dessert. The other tables were gradually emptying; the mannequins all ordered very strong coffee, several a liqueur. Only Mona and Eliane remained silent; Eliane, because she was thinking of something else; Mona, because it was her type, her *genre* to be haughty.

Her hair swept away from her white, narrow forehead and her small ears: her long earrings nearly touching her shoulders she sipped her coffee with a disdainful air. Only once, when the *blonde enfant*, having engaged in a passage of arms with the waitress and got the worst of it was momentarily discomfited and silent, Mona narrowed her eyes and smiled an astonishingly cruel smile. . . .

As soon as her coffee was drunk she got up and went out.

Anna produced a cigarette, and Georgette, perceiving instantly that here was the sportive touch, her *genre*, asked for one and lit it with a devil-may-care air. Anna eagerly passed her cigarettes round, but the Mère Pecard interfered weightily. It was against the rules of the house for the mannequins to smoke, she wheezed. The girls all lit their cigarettes and smoked. The Mère Pecard rumbled on:

'A caprice, my children. All the world knows that mannequins are capricious. Is it not so?' She appealed to the rest of the room.

As they went out Babette put her arm round Anna's waist and whispered: 'Don't answer Madame Pecard. We don't like her. We never talk to her. She spies on us. She is a camel.'

That afternoon Anna stood for an hour to have a dress draped on her. She showed this dress to a stout Dutch lady buying for the Hague, to a beautiful South American with pearls, to a silver-haired American gentleman who wanted an evening cape for his daughter of seventeen, and to a hook-nosed, odd English lady of title who had a loud voice and dressed, under her furs, in a grey jersey and stout boots.

The American gentleman approved of Anna, and said so, and Anna gave him a passionately grateful glance. For, if the *vendeuse* Jeannine had been uniformly kind and encouraging, the other, Madame Tienne, had been as uniformly

68

disapproving and had once even pinched her arm hard.

About five o'clock Anna became exhausted. The four white and gold walls seemed to close in on her. She sat on her high white stool staring at a marvellous nightgown and fighting an intense desire to rush away. Anywhere! Just to dress and rush away anywhere, from the raking eyes of the customers and the pinching fingers of Irene.

'I will one day. I can't stick it,' she said to herself. 'I won't be able to stick it.' She had an absurd wish to gasp for air.

Jeannine came and found her like that.

'It is hard at first, *hein*? . . . One asks oneself: Why? For what good? It is all *idiot*. We are all so. But we go on. Do not worry about Irene.' She whispered: 'Madame Veron likes you very much. I heard her say so.'

At six o'clock Anna was out in the rue de la Paix; her fatigue forgotten, the feeling that now she really belonged to the great, maddening city possessed her and she was happy in her beautifully cut tailor made and a beret.

MANNEQUIN

Georgette passed her and smiled; Babette was in a fur coat.

All up the street the mannequins were coming out of the shops, pausing on the pavements a moment, making them as gay and as beautiful as beds of flowers before they walked swiftly away and the Paris night swallowed them up.

VII

IN THE LUXEMBURG GARDENS

HE sat on a bench, a very depressed young man, meditating on the faithlessness of women, on the difficulty of securing money, on the futility of existence.

A little *bonne*, resting wearily first on one foot, then on the other, screamed: '*Raoul, Raoul, veux-tu te dépêcher.*' Raoul, aged two, dressed in a jade green overcoat and clutching a ball, staggered determinedly in the opposite direction. He sat down suddenly, was captured and received a slap with manly indifference.

'*Sacrés gosses!*' said the young man gazing morosely at all the other Raouls and Pierrots and Jacquelines in their brightly coloured overcoats.

He turned his head distastefully away: but instantly interest came into his eyes.

A girl was walking up the steps leading from the fountain, slowly and with a calculated grace. Her hat was as green as Raoul's overcoat, her costume extremely short, her legs . . . 'Not bad!' said the young man to himself. 'In fact . . . one may say pretty!'

The girl walked past slowly, very slowly. She looked back. The young man fidgeted, hesitated, looked at the legs. . . .

He got up and followed. She immediately walked faster and adopted an air of haughty innocence. The young man's hunting instinct awoke and he followed, twirling his little moustache determinedly. Under the trees he caught her up.

'Mademoiselle . . .'

'Monsieur . . .'

Such a waste of time, say the Luxemburg Gardens, to be morose. Are there not always Women and Pretty Legs and Green Hats.

VIII

TEA WITH AN ARTIST

IT was obvious that this was not an Anglo-Saxon: he was too gay, too dirty, too unreserved and in his little eyes was such a mellow comprehension of all the sins and the delights of life. He was drinking rapidly one glass of beer after another, smoking a long, curved pipe, and beaming contentedly on the world. The woman with him wore a black coat and skirt; she had her back to us.

I said:

'Who's the happy man in the corner? I've never seen him before.'

My companion who knew everybody answered:

'That's Verhausen. As mad as a hatter.'

'Madder than most people here?' I asked. He said:

'Oh, yes, really dotty. He has got a studio full of pictures that he will never show to anyone.'

I asked: 'What pictures? His own pictures?'

'Yes, his own pictures. They're damn good, they say.' . . . Verhausen had started out by

73

being a Prix de Rome and he had had a big reputation in Holland and Germany, once upon a time. He was a Fleming. But the old fellow now refused to exhibit, and went nearly mad with anger if he were pressed to sell anything. . . . I asked:

'A pose?'

My friend said: 'Well, I dunno. It's lasted a long time for a pose.'

He started to laugh.

'You know Van Hoyt. He knew Verhausen intimately in Antwerp, years ago. It seems he already hid his pictures up then. . . . He had evolved the idea that it was sacrilege to sell them. Then he married some young and flighty woman from Brussels, and she would not stand it. She nagged and nagged: she wanted lots of money and so on and so on. He did not listen even. So she gave up arguing and made arrangements with a Jew dealer from Amsterdam when he was not there. It is said that she broke into his studio and passed the pictures out of the window. Five of the best. Van Hoyt said that Verhausen cried like a baby when he knew. He simply sat and sobbed. Perhaps he also beat the lady. In any case she left him soon afterwards and eventually Verhausen turned up, here, in Montparnasse. The woman now with him he had picked up in some awful brothel in Antwerp. She must have been good to him, for he said now that the Fallen are the only women with souls. They will walk on the necks of all the others in Heaven . . .' And my friend concluded:

'A rum old bird. But a bit of a back number, now, of course.'

I said:

'It's a perverted form of miserliness, I suppose. I should like to see his pictures, or is that impossible? I like his face.'

My friend said carelessly:

'It's possible, I believe. He sometimes shows them to people. It's only that he will not exhibit and will not sell. I dare say Van Hoyt could fix it up.'

Verhausen's studio was in the real Latin Quarter which lies to the north of the Montparnasse district and is shabbier and not cosmopolitan yet. It was an ancient, narrow street of uneven houses, a dirty, beautiful street, full of mauve shadows. A policeman stood limply near

75

the house, his expression that of contemplative stupefaction: a yellow dog lay stretched philosophically on the cobblestones of the roadway. The concierge said without interest that Monsieur Verhausen's studio was on the *quatrième à droite*. I toiled upwards.

I knocked three times. There was a subdued rustling within. . . . A fourth time: as loudly as I could. The door opened a little and Mr. Verhausen's head appeared in the opening. I read suspicion in his eyes and I smiled as disarmingly as I could. I said something about Mr. Van Hoyt — his own kind invitation, my great pleasure.

Verhausen continued to scrutinize me through huge spectacles: then he smiled with a sudden irradiation, stood away from the door and bowing deeply, invited me to enter. The room was big, all its walls encumbered on the floor with unframed canvases, all turned with their backs to the wall. It was very much cleaner than I had expected: quite clean and even dustless. On a table was spread a white cloth and there were blue cups and saucers and a plate of gingerbread cut into slices and thickly buttered. Mr. Verhausen rubbed his hands and said with a pleased, childlike expression and in astonishingly good English that he had prepared an English tea that was quite ready because he had expected me sooner.

We sat on straight-backed chairs and sipped solemnly.

Mr. Verhausen looked exactly as he had looked in the café, his blue eyes behind the spectacles at once naive and wise, his waistcoat spotted with reminiscences of many meals. . . .

But a delightful personality — comfortable and comforting. His long, curved pipes hung in a row on the wall ; they made the whole room look Dutchly homely. We discussed Montparnasse with gravity.

He said suddenly:

'Now you have drunk your second cup of tea you shall see my pictures. Two cups of tea all English must have before they contemplate works of art.'

He had jumped up with a lightness surprising in a bulky man and with similar alacrity drew an easel near a window and proceeded to put pictures on it without any comment. They were successive outbursts of colour: it took me a little time to get used to them. I imagine that they were mostly, but not all, impressionist. But what fascinated me at first was his way of touching the canvases – his loving, careful hands.

After a time he seemed to forget that I was there and looked at them himself, anxiously and critically, his head on one side, frowning and muttering to himself in Flemish. A landscape pleased me here and there: they were mostly rough and brilliant. But the heads were very minutely painted and . . . Dutch! A woman stepping into a tub of water under a shaft of light had her skin turned to gold.

Then he produced a larger canvas, changed the position of the easel and turned to me with a little grunt. I said slowly:

'I think that is a great picture. Great art!'

. . . A girl seated on a sofa in a room with many mirrors held a glass of green liqueur. Dark-eyed, heavy-faced, with big, sturdy peasant's limbs, she was entirely destitute of lightness or grace.

But all the poisonous charm of the life beyond the pale was in her pose, and in her smouldering eyes – all its deadly bitterness and fatigue in her fixed smile.

He received my compliments with pleasure,

78

but with the quite superficial pleasure of the artist who is supremely indifferent to the opinion that other people may have about his work. And, just as I was telling him that the picture reminded me of a portrait of Manet's, the original came in from outside, carrying a string bag full of greengroceries. Mr. Verhausen started a little when he saw her and rubbed his hands again – apologetically this time. He said:

'This, Madame, is my little Marthe. Mademoiselle Marthe Baesen.'

She greeted me with reserve and glanced at the picture on the easel with an inscrutable face. I said to her:

'I have been admiring Mr. Verhausen's work.'

She said: 'Yes, Madame?' with the inflexion of a question and left the room with her string bag.

The old man said to me:

'Marthe speaks no English and French very badly. She is a true Fleming. Besides, she is not used to visitors.'

There was a feeling of antagonism in the studio now. Mr. Verhausen fidgeted and sighed restlessly. I said, rather with hesitation:

79

'Mr. Verhausen, is it true that you object to exhibiting and to selling your pictures?'

He looked at me over his spectacles, and the suspicious look, the look of an old Jew when counting his money, came again into his eyes. He said:

'Object, Madame? I object to nothing. I am an artist. But I do not wish to sell my pictures. And, as I do not wish to sell them, exhibiting is useless. My pictures are precious to me. They are precious, most probably, to no one else.'

He chuckled and added with a glint of malice in his eyes:

'When I am dead Marthe will try to sell them and not succeed, probably. I am forgotten now. Then she will burn them. She dislikes rubbish, the good Marthe.'

Marthe re-entered the room as he said this. Her face was unpowdered but nearly un-wrinkled, her eyes were clear with the shrewd, limited expression of the careful housewife – the look of small horizons and quick, hard judgments. Without the flame his genius had seen in her and had fixed for ever, she was heavy, placid and uninteresting – at any rate to me.

She said, in bad French:

'I have bought two artichokes for . . .' I did not catch how many . . . sous. He looked pleased and greedy.

In the street the yellow dog and the policeman had vanished. The café opposite the door had come alive and its gramophone informed the world that:

'Souvent femme varie
Bien fol est qui s'y fie!'

It was astonishing how the figure of the girl on the sofa stayed in my mind: it blended with the coming night, the scent of Paris and the hard blare of the gramophone. And I said to myself:

'Is it possible that all that charm, such as it was, is gone?'

And then I remembered the way in which she had touched his cheek with her big hands. There was in that movement, knowledge, and a certain sureness: as it were the ghost of a time when her business in life had been the consoling of men.

TRIO

THEY sat at a corner table in the little restaurant, eating with gusto and noise after the manner of simple-hearted people who like their neighbours to see and know their pleasures.

The man was very black — coal black, with a thick silver ring on a finger of one hand. He wore a smart grey lounge suit, cut in at the waist, and his woolly hair was carefully brushed back and brilliantined. The woman was coffee-coloured and fat. She had on the native Martinique turban, making no pretension to fashion. Her bodice and skirt gaped apart and through the opening a coarse white cotton chemise peeped innocently forth. . . . From the Antilles. . . .

Between them was the girl, apparently about fifteen, but probably much younger. She sat very close to the man and every now and then would lay her head on his shoulder for a second. . . . There was evidently much white blood in her veins: the face was charming.

She had exactly the movements of a very graceful kitten, and he, appreciative, would stop eating to kiss her . . . long, lingering kisses, and, after each one she would look round the room as if to gather up a tribute of glances of admiration and envy – a lovely, vicious little thing. . . . From the Antilles, too. You cannot think what home-sickness descended over me. . . .

The fuzzy, negress' hair was exactly the right frame for her vulgar, impudent, startlingly alive little face: the lips were just thick enough to be voluptuous, the eyes with an expression half cunning, half intelligent. She wore a very short red frock and black, patent leather shoes. Her legs were bare. Suddenly she began to sing: *J'en ai marre*, to the huge delight of the coal black man who applauded vigorously.

As she grew more excited she jumped up, swung her slim hips violently, rolled her eyes, stamped her feet, lifted her skirt. Obviously the red dress was her only garment, obviously too she was exquisite beneath it . . . supple, slender, a dancer from the Thousand and One Nights. . . .

J'en ai m-a-r-r-e.

84

The fat, coffee-coloured woman looked on peacefully, then, after a cautious glance at the *patronne* seated behind her counter:

'Keep yourself quiet, Doudou,' she said. 'Keep yourself quiet.' Then with a happy laugh:

'Mais . . . ce qu'elle est cocasse, quand même!' she said proudly.

It was because these were my compatriots that in that Montparnasse restaurant I remembered the Antilles.

MIXING COCKTAILS

THE house in the hills was very new and very ugly, long and narrow, of unpainted wood, perched oddly on high posts, I think as a protection from wood ants. There were six rooms with a verandah that ran the whole length of the house. . . . But when you went up there, there was always the same sensation of relief and coolness — in the ugly house with the beginnings of a rose garden, after an hour's journey by boat and another hour and a half on horseback, climbing slowly up. . . .

On the verandah, upon a wooden table with four stout legs, stood an enormous brass telescope. With it you spied out the steamers passing: the French mail on its way to Guadeloupe, the Canadian, the Royal Mail, which should have been stately and was actually the shabbiest of the lot. . . . Or an exciting stranger!

At night one gazed through it at the stars and pretended to be interested. . . . 'That's Venus. . . . Oh, is that Venus. . . . And that's the Southern Cross. . . .' An unloaded shotgun leant up in one corner; there were always plenty of straw rocking chairs and a canvas hammock with many cushions.

From the verandah one looked down the green valley sloping to the sea, but from the other side of the house one could only see the mountains, lovely but melancholy as mountains always are to a child.

Lying in the hammock, swinging cautiously for the ropes creaked, one dreamt. . . . The morning dream was the best — very early, before the sun was properly up. The sea was then a very tender blue, like the dress of the Virgin Mary, and on it were little white triangles. The fishing boats. . . .

A very short dream, the morning dream — mostly about what one would do with the endless blue day. One would bathe in the pool: perhaps one would find treasure. . . . Morgan's Treasure. For who does not know that, just before he was captured and I think hung at Kingston, Jamaica, Morgan buried his treasure in the Dominican mountains. . . . A wild place, Dominica. Savage and lost. Just the place for Morgan to hide his treasure in.

MIXING COCKTAILS

It was very difficult to look at the sea in the middle of the day. The light made it so flash and glitter: it was necessary to screw the eyes up tight before looking. Everything was still and languid, worshipping the sun.

The midday dream was languid too – vague, tinged with melancholy as one stared at the hard, blue, blue sky. It was sure to be interrupted by someone calling to one to come in out of the sun. One was not to sit in the sun. One had been told not to be in the sun. . . . One would one day regret freckles.

So the late afternoon was the best time on the verandah, but it was spoiled for all the rest were there. . . .

So soon does one learn the bitter lesson that humanity is never content just to differ from you and let it go at that. Never. They must interfere, actively and grimly between your thoughts and yourself – with the passionate wish to level up everything and everybody.

I am speaking to you; do you not hear? You must break yourself of your habit of never listening. You have such an absent-minded expression. Try not to look vague. . . .

So rude!

The English aunt gazes and exclaims at intervals:

'The colours. . . . How exquisite! . . . Extraordinary that so few people should visit the West Indies. . . .

'That *sea*. . . . Could anything be more lovely?'

It is a purple sea with a sky to match it. The Caribbean. The deepest, the loveliest in the world. . . .

Sleepily but tactfully, for she knows it delights my father, she admires the roses, the hibiscus, the humming birds. Then she starts to nod. She is always falling asleep, at the oddest moments. It is the unaccustomed heat.

I should like to laugh at her, but I am a well-behaved little girl. . . . Too well-behaved. . . . I long to be. . . . Like Other People! The extraordinary, ungetatable, oddly cruel Other People, with their way of wantonly hurting and then accusing you of being thin-skinned, sulky, vindictive or ridiculous. All because a hurt and puzzled little girl has retired into her shell.

The afternoon dream is a materialistic one. . . . It is of the days when one shall be plump

and beautiful instead of pale and thin : perfectly behaved instead of awkward . . . When
one will wear sweeping dresses and feathered
hats and put gloves on with ease and delight.
. . . And of course, of one's marriage: the dark
moustache and perfectly creased trousers. . . .
Vague, that.

The verandah gets dark very quickly. The
sun sets: at once night and the fireflies.

A warm, velvety, sweet-smelling night, but
frightening and disturbing if one is alone in
the hammock. Ann Twist, our cook, the
old 'Obeah' woman has told me:

'You all must'n look too much at de moon
. . .'

If you fall asleep in the moonlight you are
bewitched, it seems . . . The moon does bad
things to you if it shines on you when you
sleep . . . Repeated often . . .

So, shivering a little, I go into the room for
the comfort of my father working out his chess
problem from the *Times Weekly Edition*. Then
comes my nightly duty of mixing cocktails.

In spite of my absentmindedness I mix cocktails very well and swizzle them better . . .
(Our cocktails, in the West Indies, are drunk

frothing, and the instrument with which one froths them is called a swizzle-stick) . . . than anyone else in the house.

I measure out angostura and gin, feeling important and happy, with an uncanny intuition as to how strong I must make each separate drink.

Here then is something I can do. . . . Action, they say, is more worthy than dreaming. . . .

AGAIN THE ANTILLES

THE editor of the *Dominica Herald and Leeward Islands Gazette* lived in a tall, white house with green Venetian blinds which overlooked our garden. I used often to see him looking solemnly out of his windows and would gaze solemnly back, for I thought him a very awe-inspiring person.

He wore gold-rimmed spectacles and dark clothes always – not for him the frivolity of white linen even on the hottest day – a stout little man of a beautiful shade of coffee-colour, he was known throughout the Island as Papa Dom.

A born rebel, this editor: a firebrand. He hated the white people, not being quite white, and he despised the black ones, not being quite black. . . . 'Coloured' we West Indians call the intermediate shades, and I used to think that being coloured embittered him.

He was against the Government, against the English, against the Island's being a Crown Colony and the Town Board's new system of drainage. He was also against the Mob, against the gay and easy morality of the negroes and 'the horde of priests and nuns that over-run our unhappy Island,' against the existence of the Anglican bishop and the Catholic bishop's new palace.

He wrote seething articles against that palace which was then being built, partly by voluntary labour — until, one night his house was besieged by a large mob of the faithful, throwing stones and howling for his blood. He appeared on his verandah, frightened to death. In the next issue of his paper he wrote a long account of the 'riot': according to him it had been led by several well-known Magdalenes, then, as always, the most ardent supporters of Christianity.

After that, though, he let the Church severely alone, acknowledging that it was too strong for him.

I cannot imagine what started the quarrel between himself and Mr. Hugh Musgrave.

Mr. Hugh Musgrave I regarded as a dear, but peppery. Twenty years of the tropics and much indulgence in spices and cocktails does have that effect. He owned a big estate, just outside the town of Roseau, cultivated limes and sugar canes and employed a great deal of labour, but he was certainly neither ferocious nor tyrannical.

Suddenly, however, there was the feud in full swing.

There was in the *Dominica Herald and Leeward Islands Gazette* a column given up to letters from readers and, in this column, writing under the pseudonyms of Pro Patria, Indignant, Liberty and Uncle Tom's Cabin, Papa Dom let himself go. He said what he thought about Mr. Musgrave and Mr. Musgrave replied: briefly and sternly as befits an Englishman of the governing class. . . . Still he replied.

It was most undignified, but the whole Island was hugely delighted. Never had the *Herald* had such a sale.

Then Mr. Musgrave committed, according to Papa Dom, some specially atrocious act of tyranny. Perhaps he put a fence up where he should not have, or overpaid an unpopular overseer or supported the wrong party on the Town Board. . . . At any rate Papa Dom wrote in the next issue of the paper this passionate and unforgettable letter:

'It is a saddening and a dismal sight,' it ended, 'to contemplate the degeneracy of a stock. How far is such a man removed from the ideals of true gentility, from the beautiful description of a contemporary, possibly, though not certainly, the Marquis of Montrose, left us by Shakespeare, the divine poet and genius.

'He was a very gentle, perfect knight. . . .'

Mr. Musgrave took his opportunity:

'DEAR SIR,' he wrote,

'I never read your abominable paper. But my attention has been called to a scurrilous letter about myself which you published last week. The lines quoted were written, not by Shakespeare but by Chaucer, though you cannot of course be expected to know that, and run

He never yet no vilonye had sayde
In al his lyf, unto no manner of wight—
He was a very perfit, gentil knight.

'It is indeed a saddening and a dismal thing that the names of great Englishmen should be thus taken in vain by the ignorant of another race and colour.'

Mr. Musgrave had really written 'damn niggers.'

Papa Dom was by no means crushed. Next week he replied with dignity as follows:

'My attention has been called to your characteristic letter. I accept your correction though I understand that in the mind of the best authorities there are grave doubts, very grave doubts indeed, as to the authorship of the lines, and indeed the other works of the immortal Swan of Avon. However, as I do not write with works of reference in front of me, as you most certainly do, I will not dispute the point.

'The conduct of an English gentleman who stoops to acts of tyranny and abuse cannot be described as gentle or perfect. I fail to see that it matters whether it is Shakespeare, Chaucer or the Marquis of Montrose who administers from down the ages the much-needed reminder and rebuke.'

I wonder if I shall ever again read the *Dominica Herald and Leeward Islands Gazette.*

XII

HUNGER

LAST night I took an enormous dose of valerian to make me sleep. I have awakened this morning very calm and rested, but with very shaky hands.

It doesn't matter. I am not hungry either: that's a good thing as there is not the slightest prospect of my having anything to eat. I could of course buy a loaf, but we have been living on bread and nothing else for a long time. It gets monotonous. Also it's damned salt. . . .

Starvation — or rather semi-starvation — coffee in the morning, bread at midday, is exactly like everything else. It has its compensations, but they do not come at once. . . . To begin with it is a frankly awful business.

For the first twelve hours one is just astonished. No money: Nothing to eat. . . . *Nothing!* . . . But that's farcical. There must be something one can do. Full of practical common sense you rush about; you search for the elusive 'something.' At night you have long dreams about food.

On the second day you have a bad headache. You feel pugnacious. You argue all day with an invisible and sceptical listener.

I tell you it is *not* my fault. . . . It happened suddenly, and I have been ill. I had no time to make plans. *Can* you not see that one needs money to fight? Even with a hundred francs clear one could make plans.

I said *clear*. . . . A few hundred francs *clear*. There is the hotel to pay. Sell my clothes? . . . You cannot get any money for women's clothes in Paris. I tried for a place as a *gouvernante* yesterday. Of course I'm nervous and silly. So'd you be if . . .

Oh God! leave me alone. I don't care what you think; I don't.

On the third day one feels sick: on the fourth one starts crying very easily. . . . A bad habit that; it sticks.

On the fifth day . . .

You awaken with a feeling of detachment; you are calm and godlike. It is to attain to that state that religious people fast.

Lying in bed, my arm over my eyes, I despise, utterly, my futile struggles of the last two years. What on earth have I been making such a fuss about? What does it matter, anyway? Women are always ridiculous when they struggle.

It is like being suspended over a precipice. You cling for dear life with people walking on your fingers. Women do not only walk: they stamp.

Primitive beings, most women.

But I have clung and made huge efforts to pull myself up. . . . Three times I have . . . acquired resources! Means! Has she *means?* She has means. I have been a mannequin. I have been . . . No: not what you think . . .

No good, any of it.

Well, you are doomed.

Once down you will never get up. . . . *Did* anyone — did *any*body, I wonder, ever get up . . . Once down.

Every few months there is bound to be a crisis. Every crisis will find you weaker.

If I were Russian I should long ago have accepted Fate: had I been French I should long ago have discovered and taken the backdoor out. I mean no disrespect to the French. They are logical. Had I been . . . SENSIBLE I should have hung on to being a mannequin with what it implies. As it is, I have struggled on, not cleverly. Almost against my own will. Don't I belong to the land of Lost Causes ... England. ...

If I had a glass of wine I would drink to that: the best of toasts:

To a Lost Cause: to All Lost Causes. ...

Oh! the relief of letting go: tumbling comfortable into the abyss. ...

Not such a terrible place after all. One day, no doubt, one will grow used to it. Lots of jolly people, here. ...

No more effort. ...

Retrospection is a waste of the Fifth Day.

The best way is to spend it dreaming over some book like ... *Dash* or ... oh, *Dash*, again. ...

Especially *Dash* number one. ... There are words and sentences one can dream over for hours. ...

Luckily we have both books: too torn to be worth selling.

I love her most before she has become too vicious.

HUNGER

It is as if your nerves were strung tight. Like violin strings. Anything: lovely words, or the sound of a concertina from the street: even a badly played piano can make one cry. Not with hunger or sadness. No!

But with the extraordinary beauty of life.

I have never gone without food for longer than five days, so I cannot amuse you any longer.

XIII

DISCOURSE OF A LADY STAND-ING A DINNER TO A DOWN-AND-OUT FRIEND

DARLING, I think you are simply wonderful. I always say, if I were in your place I'd go crazy. . . . Have some more soup. . . . Soup is *so* nourishing.

(It is all very well, but she has not forgotten to rouge her lips.)

Of course, I always say one cannot judge by *appearances*. I mean that lots of people who look all right are starving, and all that, I suppose.

What did you say? . . . You cannot buy special clothes to starve in. Naturally not. But it is a question of what people *think*, is it not?

(Now she is not pleased. But is it *my* fault? A woman supposed to be starving ought not to go about in silk stockings and quite expensive shoes.)

I was with Anna at the Galerie yesterday and I saw the sweetest hat. Not *hard*. I bought it to

wear with my velvet. But they don't *go* together.
It's awful, getting clothes to go together.

(She *does* look a bit thin. I ought to ask her
to tea to-morrow. . . . No. To-morrow Albert
is coming. I dare say she is all *right*, and she is
not his type. But these people with not enough
to eat. You can't trust them with *men*. . . .
Another day. . . .)

Shall we have some more wine. . . . I wish
I could help you. Let me think. I know
somebody at Neuilly who wants a mother's
help.

(She does not like that. I knew it. It is
dreadful to try to help poor people. They will
not help themselves.)

It is a friend of Anna's really. We were talking about you the other day. I may tell you that
she is not in the least annoyed with you. Indeed
she admits that she was a little rude. But . . .
darling . . . you can't *afford* to lose your temper
like that, can you? You see, Anna and yourself
have such very different . . . let us say, tem-
peraments. She is so independent. . . . And
Peter really was annoying that day. . . . He
flirts so automatically. . . . Such a good-looking
fellow: but *what* an irritating husband. . . .

Poor Anna! It *was* not your fault. . . . But one must adapt oneself a little, mustn't one? . . . Because you are poor you are not necessarily a . . . What? What did you say? No! I never used that word. . . . You must not look at life in that way. You are too suspicious. I will ring up the woman in Neuilly. I should not do that, should I, if I did not trust you? . . . Cheer up. You will be as happy as possible. . . . (I believe she is going to cry. She irritates me. And there is that man opposite making eyes at her. Quite a good-looking man. Well, if she is that sort . . . Well, why *doesn't* she?)

Of course one has to be *some*thing in this world, hasn't one? I mean . . . There you are. . . . Either one thing or the other. . . . You will have a liqueur? *Deux kümmel, garçon.*

(I rather hate myself!)

Do you really think this hat suits me? . . . With just a *tack* in the ribbon, here, perhaps. . . . No? . . . Now don't look so sad. I will ring up Anna's friend at Neuilly to-morrow. We will fix you up. I assure you we will fix you up. They pay 150 francs a month. And keep, naturally. . . . Imagine. One hundred and fifty francs. . . . Thirty shillings. . . . Just for pocket money. . . . Good-bye, then, till you hear from Neuilly. . . .

(Poor little devil. Of course it is her own fault. That is one comfort. It is always people's own fault. . . . They lack. . . . Oh, Balance. When people lack Balance there's really nothing to be done.)

XIV

A NIGHT

ONE shuts one's eyes and sees it written: red letters on a black ground:

Le Saut dans l'Inconnu. . . . Le Saut . . .

Stupidly I think: But why in French? Of course it must be a phrase I have read somewhere. Idiotic.

I screw up my eyes wildly to get rid of it: next moment it is back again.

Red letters on a black ground.

One lies staring at the exact shape of the S.

Dreadfully tired I am too, now this beastly thing won't let me sleep. And because I can't sleep I start to think very slowly and painfully, for I have cried myself into a state of stupor.

No money: rotten. And ill and frightened to death . . . Worse!

But worst of all is the way I hate people: it is as if something in me is shivering right away from humanity. Their eyes are mean and cruel, especially when they laugh.

They are always laughing, too: always grinning. When they say something especially rotten they grin. Then, just for a second, that funny little animal, the Real Person, looks out and slinks away again . . . Furtive.

I don't belong here. I don't belong here. I must get out — must get out.

Le Saut. . . . Le Saut dans l'Inconnu.

One lies very still — staring.

Well, then . . . what?

Make a hole in the water?

In a minute I am sitting up in bed, gasping. I have imagined myself sinking, suffocating, the pain in the lungs horrible. Horrible.

Shoot oneself? . . . I begin again mechanically to plan what would happen. The revolver is in the pawnshop. For twenty francs I could. . . .

I'd sit down. No: lie down. And open my mouth. . . . That's the place: against the roof of one's mouth. How rum it would feel. And pull the trigger.

And then?

L'Inconnu: black, awful. One would fall, down, down, down for ever and ever. Falling.

Frightened. Coward. Do it when you hardly

know. Drink perhaps first half a bottle of Cognac.

No: I cannot put up a better fight than that. . . . *Be* ashamed of me.

If I had something to hold on to. Or some-body.

One friend. . . . One!

You know I can't be alone. I can't.

God, send me a friend. . . .

How ridiculous I am. How primitive. . . .

Sneering at myself I start on childish-nesses.

I imagine the man I could love. His hands, eyes and voice.

Hullo, he'll say, what's all this fuss about?

— Because I'm hurt and spoilt, and you too late. . . .

— What rot. . . . What rot!

He will buy me roses and carnations and chocolates and a pair of pink silk pyjamas and heaps of books.

He will laugh and say — but nicely:

Finished! What rot!

Just like that.

Saying the Litany to the Blessed Virgin

which I learnt at the Convent and have never forgotten.

Mater Dolorosa: Mother most sorrowful. Pray for us, Star of the Sea. Mother most pitiful, pray for us.

Ripping words.

I wonder if I dare shut my eyes now.

Ridiculous all this. Lord, I am tired. . . .

A devil of a business. . . .

IN THE RUE DE L'ARRIVÉE

HALFWAY up the Boulevard Montparnasse is a little café called the Zanzi-Bar. It is not one of these popular places swarming with the shingled and long-legged and their partners, who all wear picturesque collars and an incredibly contemptuous expression. No, it is small, half-empty, cheapish. Coffee costs five centimes less than in the Rotonde, for instance. It is a place to know of. It is not gay, except on the rare occasions when some festive soul asks the patron for the Valencia record and puts a ten centimes piece into the gramophone slot.

Here, one evening at eleven o'clock, sat a Lady drinking her fourth *fine à l'eau* and thinking how much she disliked human beings in general and those who pitied her in particular. For it was her deplorable habit, when she felt very blue indeed, to proceed slowly up the right-hand side of the Boulevard, taking a *fine à l'eau* — that is to say a brandy and soda — at every second café she passed. There are so many cafés that the desired effect could be obtained without walking very far, and by thus moving from one to the other she managed to avoid both the curious stares of the waiters and the disadvantage of not accurately knowing just how drunk she was. . . .

From which it will be very easily gathered that the Lady was an Anglo-Saxon. . . . That she was down on her luck. . . . That she lacked strength of character and was doomed to the fate of the feeble who have not found a protector. She rested her elbows on the top of the table to look at the picture of Leda and the Swan hanging opposite her. The walls of the café were covered with the canvases of hopeful artists, numbered and priced, waiting for the possible buyer. An effect of warm reds and greens and yellows and of large numbers of ladies with enormous thighs, well-developed calves and huge feet; the upper part of their bodies very slim and willowy, the faces thin and ascetic with small prim mouths.

But she was a simple soul, so her eyes strayed, puzzled and unsatisfied over these symbols of a point of view and came back to gaze steadily at the red-haired Leda, the curves of her throat and the long, white neck of the Swan lying between her breasts.

*

Into her vague dream of jade-green water and gently gliding birds with golden beaks, came a disagreeable twinge of loneliness and unhappiness. She sighed heavily, instinctively, as a dog sighs, and ordered another *Fine*. As she waited for it, she took a little mirror out of her bag and observed herself critically. From the small, blurred glass her eyes stared back at her, darkly circled, the whites slightly bloodshot, the clear look of youth going – gone.

Miss Dufreyne, for such was the Lady's name, was a weak, sentimental, very lazy, entirely harmless creature, pathetically incapable of lies or intrigue or even of self-defence – till it was too late. She was also sensual, curious, reckless, and had all her life roused a strong curiosity in men. So much for her.

Inevitably her career had been a series of jerks, very violent and very sudden, and the suddenness of the jerks – even more than their violence – had ended by exhausting her.

Nevertheless, there was still no end to her pathetic and charming illusions. She believed that Gentlemen were Different and to be trusted, that Ladies must not make a Fuss — even when drunk — and that the Lower Classes were the Lower Classes. She believed that Montparnasse, that stronghold of the British and American middle classes, was a devil of a place and what Montmartre used to be. She believed that one day she would rise to fame as a fashion artist, be rescued from her present haphazard existence and restored to a life when afternoon tea, punctually at five, toast, cakes, maid, rattle of cups in saucers would be a commonplace. Such was Miss Dufreyne's strange and secret idea of bliss.

But there she was stony-broke and with a hand that was rapidly losing its cunning, seeking oblivion in a cheap Montparnasse café. A bad stage to have reached, useless to disguise it.

Miss Dufreyne drank hastily her fifth *Fine*.

*

She sat drooping a little on the dark red leather bench, huddled in her black coat with its somewhat ragged fur collar, to all outer appearance calm, respectable, and mistress of her fate.

But over the unseen, the real Dorothy Dufreyne, a tiny shrinking thing in a vast, empty space, flowed red waves of despair, black waves of fatigue, as the brandy crept warmly and treacherously to her brain. Waves from a tremendous, booming sea. And each one would submerge her and then retreat, leaving her dazed, and as it were, gasping.

Sharp urgings to some violent deed, some inevitable fated end, and craven fear of life, and utter helpless, childish loneliness. Never before had drink, which usually warmed and uplifted her, had this effect on her. Perhaps it was because that afternoon she had passed a gentleman whom she knew intimately — very intimately indeed — and behold the gentleman had turned his head aside, and coughing nervously, pretended not to see her. . . . 'If I want to walk at all straight,' she thought suddenly, 'I'd better go now.'

She left money on the table, got up and went out in careful and dignified fashion.

Miss Dufreyne (Dolly to her friends when she had any) stepped out on to the Boulevard into the soft autumn night, and the night put out a gentle, cunning hand to squeeze her heart.

*

As soon as she turned up the side street behind the railway station which led to her hotel, she began to walk as quickly as she could. She hated that street.

It was full of cheap and very dirty hotels, of cheaper restaurants where the food smelt of oil and sweat, of coiffeurs' shops haunted by very dark men with five days' blue growth of beard. Never a pretty lady. Not the ghost of a pretty lady in these coiffeurs' shops.

Even the pharmacy at the corner looked sinister and unholy. During the day the waxen head of a gentleman with hollow eyes, thin lips and a tortured and evil expression was exhibited in the window in a little box. A legend on a card under the head read:

'I suffered from diseases of the stomach, liver, kidneys, from neurasthenia, anæmia and loss of vitality before taking the Elixir of Abbé Pierre. . . .'

A street of sordid dramas and horrible men who walked softly behind one for several steps before they spoke.

The Lady sped along, cursing the Paris pavements, almost sobered by her intense wish to get home quickly, and suddenly was aware that she was being followed.

A man was slinking up not quite alongside, a little behind her, cap pulled low over his eyes, crimson scarf knotted round his throat, hands in pockets. His silhouette looked small, almost frail, but as if he would be very quick and active like a cat. Graceful too – like a cat.

He was going to speak to her, and she felt that that night she could not bear it. 'Mademoiselle,' said the man, 'are you walking alone so late?'

'*Allez-vous en!*' she said fiercely, adding without dignity and in a voice that was almost a sob: '*Idiot!*'

Then braced herself up for the inevitable, muttered insult.

But the man, now level with her, only looked with curious, kindly, extremely intelligent eyes and passed on.

She heard him say softly, as if meditatively: '*Pauvre petite, va.*'

And because of the tone of his voice and the glance of his eyes, Miss Dufreyne felt sure that this passer-by in a sordid street knew all about her to the core of her heart and the soul of her

119

soul — the exact meaning of the tears in her eyes and the droop of her head.

It was as if those wary eyes had watched hundreds of women scold and sulk and sob and finally cry themselves into a beaten silence.

Hundreds — all precisely alike — and as if that man himself had become indifferent as Fate — but very wise and infinitely tolerant.

And instead of resenting his knowledge she felt suddenly soothed and calmed. The back of his cap and his supple slouching walk seemed to say: '*Tout s'arrangera, va!*'

And the sympathy which would have maddened her from the happy, the fortunate or the respectable, she strangely and silently accepted coming from someone more degraded than she was, more ignorant, more despised. . . .

She climbed the stairs of the hotel holding tightly to the banisters, and undressed weeping gently but not unhappily.

Her intense desire for revenge on all humanity had given place to an extraordinary clearsightedness.

For the first time she had dimly realized that only the hopeless are starkly sincere and that only the unhappy can either give or take sympathy — even some of the bitter and dangerous voluptuousness of misery.

That night Dorothy Dufreyne dreamt that she was dead and that a tall, bright angel dressed in a shabby suit and crimson scarf was bearing her to hell.

But what if it were heaven when one got there?

XVI

LEARNING TO BE A MOTHER

THERE was a large brass plate on the outside of the door:

MADAME LABORIAU
Sage-femme des Hôpitaux.
Consultations 12 à 4.

and, when one got past the concierge's loge, a steep flight of stairs. . . . Interminable, those stairs, as one mounted them, clinging to the banisters, racked with pain. Then there was another door with a smaller plate: *Sage-femme*.

Inside there was a turmoil — loud voices, mewing of babies, a warm smell of blankets, a woman moaning. For Madame Laboriau, being a qualified maternity nurse, must, according to the law, keep one large room for overflowings from the hospitals. . . . I see the women as I pass the open door — three of them, one already crazy with pain, the others watching her with white, curious faces. I turn away my head quickly.

A long passage and I am in my own room.

Fortunate me! I have been able to buy the right to moan in privacy.

It is extraordinary how that electric light hurts one. If only I could get them to put it out. Painfully I try to remember the French for light. . . . '*Lumière . . . Éteindre la lumière.*' They do not understand and I begin to cry weakly.

Madame Laboriau sponges my forehead, looks at me with an expert eye. I look up at her and say again:

'*Anesthésique. . . . On m'a promis. . . .*'

She smiles and pats my hand.

'La la la la,' she says as she hurries away.

I am alone again with the light – yellow and cruel. But now there are two of them, elongated, and round them a quivering halo.

I watch the halo as the giant pain takes me up and squeezes me tighter, tighter, tighter.

*

'*Regardez,*' says Mme. Laboriau, '*comme il est beau votre fils. . . .*' Look how beautiful is your son!

I look and think weakly: Poor hideous little thing!

Oh do take it away, I say fretfully, and then: Thirsty!

Colette came as soon as I could see visitors, laden of course with flowers and grapes. She had been a friend of my husband and visited me when I first came to Paris, I think out of polite inquisitiveness. . . . But we were curious about each other, so we had gradually become intimate. . . . She had all the qualities. She was beautiful, gay – and she read Tolstoi. Only to put herself to sleep it is true – still she read him. I spent a night at her flat once and actually saw her doing it.

She was more than a Parisienne: she was a Montmartroise, which is a Parisienne raised to the *n*th power.

And generous. . . . She was contemplating marriage, but, I believe, with misgivings.

Well, she came to see the baby and to coo at it. I had to account for my lack of enthusiasm by saying that I had wanted a girl. . . .

'*Ah, mais, non, par exemple!*' she said decidedly, 'A man, a son! that is something. But a woman . . . another *pauvre miserable*. . . . Michel? Is he not proud? And pleased?'

125

I told her: yes. Very pleased. Very proud. And his name, the poor little cabbage?

'Robert,' I said rather shamefacedly.

'Robayre, *bon*. But I thought it was to be Michel!'

I had meant to call him Michael. Robert had slipped out.

It had been like this:

A couple of days after he was born a little, wizened, dried-up man had come to see me — somebody connected with the Mairie. He was smiling and courteous at first.

Was I married — Yes.

My husband's name?

I read carefully from my marriage lines which I had under my pillow: Michel Ivan . . .

Astonishing to see how suddenly the smile left his face.

'Ivan . . . then . . . Your husband is a Russian. A Bolshevik, no doubt!'

I said that my husband was French though born in Russia.

'Ivan . . . Ivan . . . c'est Bolshevik, ça,' he muttered unconvincedly.

Then sharply: 'The name of this child, Madame?'

126

I stared at him, not being prepared for this. 'The child's name, Madame?' he asked even more sharply.

And, thoroughly frightened, I stammered the first name that came into my head: 'Robert!'

Alone with my son I said to him remorsefully: 'At first I don't like you and now I've been and called you Robert. You poor little devil.'

There it was. I did not like him. I had been too much hurt. I was too tired.

I kept my feelings a profound secret, but with all my efforts I could not bring myself to kiss him. . . . I was thankful that he slept nearly all the time. I spent the days sleeping, reading a book called *Saadha la Marocaine*, talking to Mme. Laboriau whenever she had time to sit with me.

I had grown to admire her. It was impossible not to admire anyone so calm, so efficient, so entirely mistress of herself and of her work. . . . She was fat, with steady, clever, blue eyes, and, underneath her overalls, she wore brightly coloured dresses of velvet. Her hands were small, white, and extraordinarily deft. . . . With one of them she would lift the baby up, catching him in the middle somewhere, and the little animal, recognizing the touch of the expert, would stop crying at once.

She said with regard to my want of enthusiasm about him:

'That is always so. That will come. That will come. You are still weak. Besides, one must learn.'

She sat comfortably down and began to talk. Suddenly from the next rooms came moans and shrieks.

'*Ça y est!*' she exclaimed, 'the moment I sit down of course.'

'Perhaps,' I said timidly, 'she is suffering very much.'

'Bah. . . . Like you: like me. . . . But the less they pay the more noise they make. That is fated but it is extraordinary.'

'Jésus! Jésus!' screamed the woman in the next room. 'Mon Dieu . . . Mon Dieu . . . Mon Dieu . . .'

She moved towards the door, serene, unhurried, and I pulled the sheet over my head to shut out the shrieks.

What lies people tell about maternity! Sacred Motherhood! La Femme Sacrée!

128

Well, there is la Femme Sacrée in the next room. Horrible World. . . .

So I must have slept.

*

I woke up during the night to hear the little wail of Robert. Because it was a little wail I lifted him out of his crib and held him in my arms. He made a sad, complaining noise that almost stopped as I rocked him backwards and forwards. How warm the room was! How silent! Very far away a dog barking, the horn of a taxi.

Suddenly I realized that I was happy.

There was a nightlight burning. He opened his eyes and looked straight into mine. His were set slantwise, too, and I imagined they looked sad.

He was tied up in the French way like a Red Indian papoose, only his head out of the bundle. I shall dress him differently when we get home.

Little thing! I must kiss him.

Perhaps that is why he looks sad — because his mother never has kissed him.

XVII

THE BLUE BIRD

ON that afternoon Carlo and I sat in the Café du Dôme drinking kümmel. The room was comparatively empty, for the weather being hot the Dômites were gathered on the terrace.

There were the usual number of young gentlemen with high voices, carefully shabby trousers, jerseys, caressing gestures, undulating hips, and the usual number of the stony broke sitting haughtily behind *cafés-crème*. The bald waiter with the lecherous eyes trod to and fro, disdainful and flat-footed; the end of a gay scarf floated in the breeze; the high, sharp voice of a respectable English woman discoursed of her uncle the bishop and her hatred of hysteria.

Most of the women were ugly that afternoon. The unpainted faces looked bald and unfinished, the painted – ochre powder, shadowed eyelids, purple lips – were like cruel stains in the sunlight.

In the corner, to redeem humanity, sat one lovely creature, her face framed by a silver turban. Wisps of woolly hair peeped out from beneath it – a nigger – what a pity. Why a pity?

One becomes impressionistic to excess after the third kümmel!

'Another, Carlo?'

'Horrible extravagance!' said Carlo in her deep voice.

Carlo is a mass of contradictions. Her voice is as deep as a man's; her shoulders and hips narrow as those of a fragile schoolgirl, her eyes brown and faithful like a dog's (hence her name). Her mouth is bitter and tormented. But for her mouth one would not guess that she is a failure, a tragedy, one of the tragedies of Montparnasse.

Montparnasse is full of tragedy – all sorts – blatant, hidden, silent, voluble, quick, slow – even lucrative – A tragedy can be lucrative, I assure you.

On any day of the week you may catch sight of the Sufferers, white-faced and tragic of eye – having a drink in the intervals of expressing themselves – pouring out their souls and exposing them hopefully for sale, that is to say.

Everybody knows Carlo, and nobody blames

her, and she is such a *nice* woman really and such a hopeless case.

Poor soul, she loved a Bad Man — and there you are. Such a pity!

I believe her real name is Margaret Tomkins and her birthplace doesn't matter — London probably. But she left England ten years ago when she was about seventeen, and wandered all over Europe, first with the nondescript Greek whom she had married for some extraordinary reason, possibly because she was bored — and then with the Bad Man. She met the Bad Man first in Bucharest. They finally arrived in Paris where Carlo started a desultory career as an artist's model, and came to live in Montparnasse. The Bad Man stayed over on the other side of the river, but he would swoop down and carry her off at intervals. People said he took all her money — regardless of how it was earned — but Carlo always swore solemnly that this wasn't true.

On the contrary, she said, he spent all his on her — recklessly.

She had a very varied existence anyway, but has never lost the look of a country clergyman's daughter — which I believe she is. She dresses unimaginatively, with occasional outbreaks into some too vivid colour. She wore that day a red straw hat and in its shadow her face looked very pale, her eyes so clearly brown that they were almost yellow.

She said suddenly: 'Oh, thank God, thank God, it's hot. There are only about two hot days every year. This is one of them. Lovely!'

I agreed without so much enthusiasm. I've never learned the art of sitting absolutely still, divinely lazy in the golden sun for hours at a time and dreaming vaguely.

Carlo had it, but she had lived so long in hot places and wasn't quite English to start with.

She rested her chin on her hand and gazed at all the familiar faces outside without seeing them.

*

She said:

'One night last summer when it was hot like this, I was happy. People say you are never utterly happy — but I was.'

She spoke in a low voice.

I was surprised.

Carlo so seldom talked about herself, and never of her loves, which were necessarily many, poor dear. That alone made her unique in Montparnasse, unique amongst women, I think.

She said:

'You see, I hadn't heard from Paul for several weeks, and I was awfully worried.' (Paul was the Bad Man.) 'And then I got a wire from him. He was at Barbizon and he asked me to come. You know Barbizon in Fontainebleau Forest?'

I said: 'Yes. Classical for lovers, my dear.'

'Well,' said Carlo, 'and I went.'

(Of course – you poor devil of a blind and infatuated creature – of course you went.)

'And I got down towards evening and I took a cab from Melun to the hotel. I was simply miserable in the cab. Miserable! You know how one is. I'd such a horrible fear that I was never going to see Paul again – he was one of those people whom one adores and whom one is never sure of because they seem marked out . . . fated . . . do you know what I mean? No? Well, there are people like that.

'The bedroom at the hotel was full of flowers and all the windows were open – so many windows. It was like being outside.

'And Paul said:

' "Carlo, don't let's talk now – after dinner,

135

after dinner! Let's be happy now. Let's forget everything. Have you brought your little black dress? Put it on.''

'So I shut my eyes and I kissed him and I didn't ask a single question — not one, not even if he had money. After all, it didn't matter, for I had some.'

(I repressed a movement of indignation and drank some kümmel. Poor, poor Carlo!)

She went on:

'We had dinner outside on the terrace. The forest begins only a few yards away — the hotel is on the edge of it — and someone has stuck up a sort of shed where people shoot with little guns at something — I don't know what — But we sat with our backs to that, of course.

'I never even noticed the other people. I don't know if the place was full or empty. We ate everything good and drank Sauternes, and I began to feel happy.

'Paul said:

' "Now, we're going into the forest — and will talk, if you like. . . ."

'You know it's extraordinary; the forest near Barbizon is absolutely empty at night. You'd think that all the people from the hotels would drift there after dinner, but they don't. It's empty and still and wonderful. We left the path after a while. The trees got thicker and everything was utterly silent. If I'd been alone I should have been afraid, for I think trees get strange at night, don't you? I love them – but they're strange. I'm sure they are more alive than people imagine. . . .

'And Paul said:

' "We're quite safe here. We're absolutely alone – I'll make a bed for you with my coat."

'He said:

' "Carlo!"

'Do you know how men's eyes look sometimes, as if they were begging desperately and . . . and childishly somehow! . . .

'You can't think how white his face looked under the trees – And his eyes – they had little lamps in them.

'I thought: Paul looks quite mad.

'I kissed his eyes to make them peaceful.

'And as I was doing that a nightingale began to sing – to sing and sing.

'I was so happy – I've never felt like that before. I never will feel like that again.

'I whispered to Paul: "Wouldn't it be wonder-

137

ful to die now?" He said: "Carlo, do you mean that? Have you the courage? I'd hold you tight — you wouldn't feel anything."

'I sat up and looked at him and he said: "Have you the courage, Carlo? Tell me — have you?"

'And somehow I was frightened of his eyes and I said: "There's a mosquito — you said there weren't many this year — but there's one."

'It's funny, sometimes a devil talks with one's tongue!

'I wanted to say: "Yes, kill me. It would be worth living to die like this!"

'And instead I said that about the mosquitoes.

'He helped me up and he said: "Let's go back to the hotel."

'All the way home he only spoke once. He said: "Don't worry about money. I've got enough to pay the bill with in my pocket-book."

'He . . .'

Carlo stopped and suddenly began to cry. 'Oh, God, what a fool I was — what a fool! To have been so close to a sweet death and to have pushed it away! Because I was frightened. And went on living — to be a wreck! And to grow old — and to be the butt of a lot of thick fools — I clung on to mean, silly life. Oh! God . . . That night, you know, when he got up to . . . to go and kill himself, he must have kissed me. . . . In my sleep I felt him kiss me.'

I gave her my handkerchief in sympathetic silence. Hers was so small. . . .

Poor Carlo! The first time I'd ever heard her version. The generally accepted one was that the Bad Man had been a Bad Man to the end — and being wanted by the police for something pretty serious he had shot himself one night at Barbizon, 'having first carefully dragged that unfortunate girl into the business, couldn't even kill himself decently.'

Life is really unsatisfactory and puzzling — very.

All Carlo's friends thought — or pretended to think — that being finally quit of him she'd go up in the world like a skyrocket. And instead of that she went to pieces — absolutely to pieces. She resented fiercely all the well-meant efforts to rouse her to some sense of duty towards life.

There you are! And there she was — the tragedy of Montparnasse — called 'Poor Carlo' by the charitable, and 'that awful woman' by the others. . . .

Now she powdered her face, pulled her hat over her eyes and got up.

She said:

'Well, I've got to go and meet my Arab. D'you know my Arab? He's got a beauty spot on his left cheek like somebody out of the Thousand and One Nights. Awfully good-looking. But a bit of a rotter on the quiet, I should think. . . . Good-bye, my dear – sorry I cried – idiotic to cry.'

I watched her red hat in the sun as she crossed the Boulevard.

XVIII

THE GREY DAY

ONE of those cold, heavy days in spring – a hard sky with a glare behind the cloud, all the new green of the trees hanging still and sullen.

A day without joy or romance, or tenderness – when joy and romance and tenderness seem impossible, unthinkable – ridiculous illusions – and sadness itself is only a pale ghost.

The poet walked solemnly along the Boulevard Raspail and longed for the sight of a pretty woman – a useless creature with polished nails, expensive scent and the finest of silk stockings – marked and warranted – For Ornament Fragile –

They cheer one up sometimes. . . . But not one was to be seen.

All the women he met marched heavily with sensible feet and carried parcels. One even held a green broom and looked as if she'd like to sweep the poet out of existence with it.

He groaned, rushed into a café, and ordered a drink. He felt like the Princess who had to spin a beautiful garment out of nothing at all, or have her head cut off.

Imagine being a poet in a world like this!

Imagine being obliged to write one poem (at least) every morning!

Then his despair faded again to greyness in that dark, quiet café, where two men with hooked noses and greasy, curly hair, played draughts.

He shut his eyes and tried hard to think of blue seas in the sunshine, of the white, supple arms of a dancer dressed in red – of the throb that lives in a violin and the movement of flowers in the wind.

It was quite useless.

Besides, flowers have stupid faces and so have dancers for the matter of that.

He ordered another drink.

It was a grey day – between heat and cold, summer and winter, youth and age.

The poet meditated on all the sensible people in the world, on all the lumps of beef waiting to be eaten, on all the children waiting to have their noses blown – on the Ugliness of Virtue and the Sad Reaction after Vice.

On Mornings. On Getting Up.

THE GREY DAY

He was a young poet and he realized that before him in all probability stretched endlessly thousands of mornings. On every one of which he'd have to get up and bathe. No, he could not bathe, for he was poor and lived in Paris. Get up and wash then — slowly — bit by bit.

It was the last straw.

The poet paid for his drinks. . . .

XIX

THE SIDI

IT was four o'clock on a Sunday afternoon.
Soon a bell would warn the prisoners that
officially it was night and time to sleep in the
prison of the Santé.

No. 54 made his simple preparations for
repose. He spread his mattress on the floor, for
the bars of the iron bed were broken, and to lie
on it was torture. Then he stretched himself out
fully dressed, eyes wide open, staring at the
damp, dirty white walls of his cell. Further and
further the walls seemed to recede into the
shadow. . . .

His neighbour on the right began a persistent
drumming on the wall: Tap, tap, tap, tap, tap,
tap, tap, tap. . . .

A code, doubtless; it happened every night.

No. 54 did not answer. The drumming became faster, redoubled its vigour for a time,
then stopped slowly as if regretfully.

A heavy step followed by someone walking
quickly and lightly. No. 54 heard the door on

the left open with loud creaking of its rusty hinges. He heard the warder's voice explaining the way the bed must be made and unmade, the exhortations to be of good behaviour, obedient, orderly, clean — above all clean: the same exhortations he had heard when he had been entombed in his own cell, the walls of which swarmed with vermin, oozed with a black damp.

'*Tiens*, a new one,' thought No. 54.

He began to picture the new one in the obscurity, preparing to lie down on his horrible bed, the mattress stained, the sheets grey and damp, the coverlet foul. . . .

No. 54 dozed. But in the middle of the night he was awakened by a monotonous chant, a plaintive, minor chant, tuneless, wordless, without other rhythm than that of a high, sharp note at intervals.

It sounded like a dirge in the obscene darkness, and the silent walls of the prison began to wake. The other prisoners were banging with angry fists for silence. But the chant persisted, a wave of sound without end or beginning — an obsession.

When it stopped at last No. 54 was unable to

146

sleep and he lay making conjectures about his neighbour for the rest of the night. A madman, perhaps — there were madmen in the prison — or a habitué who wanted to show that he did not give a dam.

Not that he had sounded joyful or even defiant — it was more like someone praying. And suddenly No. 54 remembered the days before the war when it was fashionable to represent scenes from Moroccan life on the stages of Paris music-halls, and the Moroccan troops on the French front in 1914.

He thought:

'Of course, a Sidi, a Bicot.'

Why not? One of those Arabs who came over in masses during the war, who stayed in France the war over 'to become good Frenchmen.' They stayed, naively hoping to make fortunes out of the lowest and the worst paid work, living in colonies in the popular quarters of Paris, always at odds with the law which they did not understand, and with the 'Roumis' whose wives and daughters they coveted in defiance of Allah — drinking wine in floats notwithstanding the Koran.

One of those Arabs — ragged, verminous,

thieves, quarrelsome. That was it. That monotonous complaint in the night — he had already heard it when the Bicots on the front chanted their invocations to Allah, the Compassionate.

During the morning exercise No. 54 caught sight of his neighbour. He was an Arab, but not an Arab of the expected type, haggard with privations and drink, covered with vermin, devoured by a secret malady. This was quite a young man and beautiful as some savage Christ. A head sharply cut, as it were, out of ivory and ebony, two long, very black eyes under heavy eyelids and long eyelashes, a red-lipped mouth with teeth marvellously white and even in the emaciated, copper-coloured face. Among his squalid companions he looked like a chief, a king.

As the prisoners descended the staircase in Indian file the Sidi turned:

'You — tobacco?' he demanded.

'Yes,' answered No. 54, deftly handing him a little tobacco hidden in the hollow of his palm.

At the turn of the staircase a warder bawled:

'Ah! You there! You, le Bicot, forward! Eyes front!'

The Sidi shrugged his shoulders disdainfully and spat on the ground.

As soon as they were out of the sight of the warder he spoke again:

'Me — not guilty — me not know why in prison — Me sick, very sick.'

'They all say that,' thought No. 54. 'They don't understand, naturally, poor devils.'

'You a long time here?' asked the Sidi again.

But another guardian appeared making any answer impossible.

About ten o'clock, after the distribution of the morning soup, at the hour when all the prisoners whose turn it was to appear at the Palais de Justice had left their cells and the day's canteen had been given out, the Sidi began to chant again: the long, guttural complaint filled No. 54's cell, made there as it were a thick curtain of melancholy which smothered the power of thought. It was lugubrious as the howling of a dog in a still country night, and it broke off suddenly without an end, without a final note.

A tap on the wall — one, two, three taps. In the prisoners' code: letter C No. 54 rapped in answer. The Sidi knocked seventeen times — Q — Then eight times — H.

No. 54 did not reply. C-Q-H did not make a word. The Arab could not know the letters of the alphabet, useless after all to try to communicate with him.

About four o'clock in the afternoon the Sidi intoned his prayer, always the same, the only recognizable word:

Allah — Allah — Allah!

It was a persecution, something relentless and terrible.

He chanted regularly at stated hours. At night the sound dragged like an uneasy and agonizing dream; in the day it was fierce, obstinate, high, shrill above all the noises of the cells:

Allah — Allah — Allah! . . .

*

Every morning No. 54 saw the Arab. Every morning they had the same conversation:

'You — tobacco?'

'Yes.'

'Me — not guilty — me not know why in prison.'

One morning the Sidi was absent when the prisoners went for their morning exercise.

'He must be at the Palais de Justice,' thought No. 54.

(For it is at the Santé that the accused spend the time, sometimes months, which elapses between their arrest and their trial at the Palais de Justice.)

But back in the cell he heard a warder unlock his neighbour's door.

'*Comment, salaud*, in bed! Espèce de sale Bicot! Get up and get a move on you!'

'Very sick!' moaned the Arab.

'Sick! Couldn't you have said so this morning? Get up! Allez ! Oust!'

'Sick,' repeated the Sidi.

The warder's voice swelled with rage and pompous irritation:

'Wait a bit — I'll give you sick, you lazy devil you — *Tu te f — du monde* — Wait a bit, you lousy nigger — *espèce de c —*'

The dull thud of a blow — another — another. . . . Not a sound from the Arab. Then a chair overturned, a heavy fall.

The hinges of the door creaked again:

'You want to stay on the floor; well, stay on the floor, but leave the bed alone or I'll give you bed, *salaud.*'

The door of the cell shut, the heavy clump of hobnailed boots along the corridor — silence.

That day the Sidi did not chant, but his life seemed to be draining itself away in a plaintive, endless litany of moans.

When the hour came for food to be served:

'*Tiens,*' said the warder, 'he is still on the floor, the *salaud* — He'd better be careful — *faut pas qu'il m'em —*!'

And to the auxiliary who was serving a quarter of a tin bowl of uneatable rice soup to each prisoner:

'The Bicot doesn't need to eat. *Il peut crever!*'

All that night the frail, thin, moaning sound continued with the regularity of water dripping from a leak. Towards morning it stopped.

'Gone to sleep, poor devil,' thought No. 54 with relief.

At seven o'clock, when the warder came to inspect the beds, there were again loud curses from the direction of the Sidi's cell.

Then a cry — half astounded, half annoyed:

'*M —, il a clamsé, le Bicot!*' (He's kicked the bucket.)

Then No. 54, horrified, knew that his beautiful neighbour was dead. He began to imagine those big, laughing eyes which had been full of images of the vivid colours and the hot light of

Morocco, closing on the cold, sombre walls of a French prison, the untidy, dirty bed, the fat fist – black-nailed, the red, furious face and the loose mouth that spat curses of a 'Roumi' functionary.

XX

AT THE VILLA D'OR

SARA OF MONTPARNASSE had arrived that afternoon at the Villa d'Or, and it was now 9.30
p.m.; dinner was just over, it was the hour of
coffee, peace, optimism.

From the depths of a huge arm-chair Sara
admired the warmly lovely night which looked
in through the open windows, the sea, the moon,
the palms — the soft lighting of the room.

The very faint sound of music could be heard
from the distant Casino at intervals, and on the
sofa opposite Mrs. Robert B. Valentine re-
clined, dressed in a green velvet gown with
hanging sleeves lined with rosy satin. Mr.
Robert B. Valentine, the Boot-Lace King,
sprawled in another huge arm-chair, and five
Pekinese were distributed decoratively in the
neighbourhood of Mrs. Valentine. It might
have been the Villa of the Golden Calf.

'And very nice too,' thought Sara.

Charles came in to take away the coffee-tray,
and to present Mr. Valentine with a large, blue
book.

Charles was like the arm-chairs, English. He was also, strange to say, supple, handsome, carefully polite. But then Charles was definitely of the lower classes (as distinct from the middle).

'The chef is there, sir,' said he – and 'Anything more, Madame?'

'Nothing, Charles,' said Mrs. Valentine with a hauteur touched with sweetness.

Charles retreated with grace, carrying the tray. He looked as though he enjoyed the whole thing immensely. His good looks, his supple bow from the waist, his livery . . .

'It must be fun,' thought Sara, 'to be butler in a place where everything is so exactly like a film.'

Mrs. Valentine's daughter of Los Angeles, Cal., was the most famous of movie stars. She received a thousand love-letters per month. In London she was mobbed when she went out. . . . There was a glamour as distinct from money over the household. . . .

Mr. Valentine put on horn-rimmed spectacles and opened the blue book which told of *Risotto of lobster*, of *bécassine glacée sur lac d'or*, of green peppers stuffed with rice.

After a prolonged study of it he announced

like some saint turning his back on the false glitter of this world:

'He's got haricots verts down for to-morrow, darling – wouldn't you like some rice for a change?'

Mr. Valentine was a vegetarian, a teetotaller, a non-smoker, an example of the law of compensation like most American millionaires.

Mrs. Valentine moved a little impatiently on her sofa, and through her dignified charm pierced a slight fretfulness.

'I'm just dead sick of rice, Bobbie,' said she. 'Couldn't we have some ham for a change?'

'He says he can't get a ham,' said Mr. Valentine doubtfully. 'He says he'll have to send to Paris for a ham.'

The lady sat up suddenly and announced with energy that it was all nonsense, that she had seen lovely hams in the corner shop in Cannes – that anyone who couldn't get a ham in Cannes couldn't get one anywhere.

'I'll speak to him, darling,' Mr. Valentine told her soothingly.

He got up and walked alertly out. He wore a purple smoking suit and under the light his perfectly bald head shone as if it were polished. He was extremely like some cheerful insect with long, thin legs.

When he had gone, Mrs. Valentine leant back on to her sofa and half closed her eyes. She was such a slender lady that, sunk into the soft cushions she seemed ethereal, a creature of two dimensions, length and breadth, without any thickness. Her shoes were of gold brocade and round her neck glittered a long necklace of green beads with which she fidgeted incessantly — her hands being white and well manicured, but short, energetic and capable, with broad, squat nails.

A Romantic, but only on the surface; also an active and energetic patroness of the Arts, fond of making discoveries in Montparnasse and elsewhere.

So Mr. Pauloff, a little Bulgarian who lived in Vienna, occupied a sumptuous bedroom on the second floor. He painted.

Sara, who sang, was installed on the third floor, though, as she was a female and relatively unimportant, her room was less sumptuous.

*

'It makes me feel sad, that music in the night,' declared Mrs. Valentine. 'The man who is singing at the Casino this week is Mr. van den

Cleef's gardener. Isn't it just too strange? A Russian — a prince or something. Yes. And he only gets — what does a gardener get? I don't know — so he sings at the Casino in the evening. Poor man! And so many of them — all princes or generals or Grand Dukes. . . . Of course most unreliable. . . . Why, my dear Miss Cohen, I could tell you stories about the Russians on the Riviera — Well! Strange people — very strange. Not like us. Always trying to borrow money.'

She went on to talk of the Russian character, of her tastes in music, of Mr. Valentine's eighteenth-century bed, of the emptiness of life before she became a spiritualist, of automatic writing.

'Yes, yes,' said Sara patiently at intervals.

After all, this was a tremendous reaction from Paris. In Paris one was fear-hunted, insecure, one caught terrifying glimpses of the Depths and the monsters who live there. . . . At the Villa d'Or life was something shallow . . . that tinkled meaninglessly . . . shallow but safe.

Through Mrs. Valentine's high-pitched drawl she strained her ears to hear some faint sound of the sea and imagined the silken caress of the water when she would bathe next morning.

Bathing in that blue jewel of a sea would be a voluptuousness, a giving of oneself up. And coming out of it one would be fresh, purified from how many desecrating touches.

Poor Sara . . . also a Romantic!

As Mrs. Valentine was describing the heroism of a famous American dancer who acted as a secret service agent during the war and averted catastrophe to the Allies by swallowing important documents at the right moment, Mr. Pauloff and Mr. Valentine came in.

'Well, I've told him about that ham, darling,' said the Boot-Lace King brightly.

He added in a lower tone: 'Yes, nood, but not too nood, Mr. Pauloff.'

'There will be a drapery,' the Bulgarian assured him.

Mr. Pauloff had painted Mrs. Valentine two years ago surrounded by her Pekinese, and made her incredibly beautiful. Then he had painted Mr. Valentine with exquisite trousers and the rest, brown boots and alert blue eye.

He was now decorating the panels of Mr. Valentine's bedroom door with figures of little ladies. And a tactful drapery was to float round the little ladies' waists. After all he had been a court painter and he had learned to be miraculously tactful. A polite smile was always carved — as it were — on his ugly little face; in his brown, somewhat pathetic eyes was a look of strained attention.

'In courts and places like that,' as Mr. Valentine said, 'they learn nice manners. Well, I guess they just have to. . . .'

'I understand, I quite understand,' the artist said diffidently, but with finality, 'I will drape the figures.'

Then he handled a bundle of press-cuttings which he was holding to Sara and asked if she would read them aloud.

'You have so nice, so charming a voice, Miss Sara.'

Sara, overcome by this compliment, proceeded to read the cuttings which were from the English papers of fifteen years before.

'Mr. Yvan Pauloff, the famous Bulgarian artist . . .'

'At a sale of Mr. Yvan Pauloff's paintings . . .'

As Sara read Mrs. Valentine closed her eyes and seemed to sleep, but Mr. Valentine, crossing his legs, listened with great attention; as to the artist himself, he heard it all with a pleased smile, fatuous but charming.

Then he went — radiant — to fetch some photographs of his most celebrated pictures. Mr. Valentine said quickly:

'You see, deary, there you are; he is a great artist. His name on a picture means something — means dollars.'

'Dollars aren't Art, Bobbie,' answered Mrs. Valentine loftily.

Mr. Valentine muttered something, and walking to the window surveyed the view with a proprietor's eyes.

'Come out on the terrace and look at the stars, Miss Sara,' said he. 'Now that star there, it's green, ain't it?'

'Quite green,' she agreed politely, following him out.

He glanced sideways at her, admiring the curves of her figure — he liked curves — the noble and ardent sweep of her nose — that saving touch of Jewish blood!

He proceeded to pour out his soul to the sympathetic creature:

'My wife's always talking about Art. She thinks I don't understand anything about it.

Well, I do. Now, for instance: Bottles — the curve of a bottle, the shape of it — just a plain glass bottle. I could look at it for hours. . . . I started life in a chemist's shop — I was brought up amongst the bottles. Now the pleasure I get in looking at a bottle makes me understand artists. . . . D'you get me?'

'Why, that's absolutely it,' said Sara warmly in response to the note of appeal in his voice. 'You understand perfectly.'

'Would you like to come to Monte with me Sunday?' asked Mr. Valentine in a lower tone, grasping Sara's arm above the elbow. 'I'll teach you to play roulette.'

'Yes, it would be fun,' said Sara without a great deal of enthusiasm.

From inside the Villa came the sweet and mocking music of 'La Bergère Légère.'

'And there's my wife playing the Victrola — Time for my billiards,' chirped Mr. Valentine.

He went briskly up the steps and hauled away an unwilling Mr. Pauloff to the billiard-room.

'Sometimes,' said Mrs. Valentine to Sara, 'I play the Victrola for hours all by myself when Bobbie is in the billiard-room, and I think how strange it is that lovely music — and voices of people who are dead — like Caruso — coming out of a black box. Their voices — Themselves in fact — And I just get frightened to death — terrified. I shut it up and run up the stairs and ring like mad for Marie.'

The marble staircase of the Villa d'Or was dim and shadowy, but one or two electric lights were still lit near the famous (and beautiful) portrait of Mrs. Valentine.

'When I see that portrait,' said the lady suddenly, 'I'm glad to go to bed sometimes.'

*

In her huge bedroom where the furniture did not quite match, where over the bed hung a picture representing a young lady and gentleman vaguely Greek in costume, sitting on a swing with limbs entwined in a marvellous mixture of chastity and grace — this was a relic of the days before Mrs. Valentine had learned to appreciate Picasso — Sara opened the windows wide and looked out on the enchanted night, then sighed with pleasure at the glimpse of her white, virginal bathroom through the open door — the bath-salts, the scents, the crystal bottles.

She thought again: 'Very nice too, the Villa d'Or.'

XXI

LA GROSSE FIFI

'The sea,' said Mark Olsen, 'is exactly the colour of Rickett's blue this morning.'

Roseau turned her head to consider the smooth Mediterranean.

'I like it like that,' she announced, 'and I wish you wouldn't walk so fast. I loathe tearing along, and this road wasn't made to tear along anyhow.'

'Sorry,' said Mark, 'just a bad habit.'

They walked in silence, Mark thinking that this girl was a funny one, but he'd rather like to see a bit more of her. A pity Peggy seemed to dislike her — women were rather a bore with their likes and dislikes.

'Here's my hotel,' said the funny one. 'Doesn't it look awful?'

'You know,' Mark told her seriously, 'you really oughtn't to stay here. It's a dreadful place. Our *patronne* says that it's got a vile reputation—someone got stabbed or something, and the *patron* went to jail.'

'You don't say!' mocked Roseau.

'I do say. There's a room going at the *pension*.'

'Hate *pensions*.'

'Well, move then, move to St. Paul or Juan les Pins – Peggy was saying yesterday. . . .'

'Oh Lord!' said Roseau rather impatiently, 'my hotel's all right. I'll move when I'm ready, when I've finished some work I'm doing. I think I'll go back to Paris – I'm getting tired of the Riviera, it's too tidy. Will you come in and have an aperitif?'

Her tone was so indifferent that Mark, piqued, accepted the invitation though the restaurant of that hotel really depressed him. It was so dark, so gloomy, so full of odd-looking, very odd-looking French people with abnormally loud voices even for French people. A faint odour of garlic floated in the air.

'Have a Deloso,' said Roseau. 'It tastes of anis,' she explained, seeing that he looked blank. 'It's got a kick in it.'

'Thank you,' said Mark. He put his sketches carefully on the table, then looking over Roseau's head his eyes became astonished and fixed. He said:

'Oh my Lord! What's that?'

166

'That's Fifi,' answered Roseau in a low voice and relaxing into a smile for the first time.

'Fifi! Of course — it would be — Good Lord! — Fifi!' His voice was awed. 'She's — she's terrific, isn't she?'

'She's a dear,' said Roseau unexpectedly.

Fifi was not terrific except metaphorically, but she was stout, well corseted — her stomach carefully arranged to form part of her chest. Her hat was large and worn with a rakish sideways slant, her rouge shrieked, and the lids of her protruding eyes were painted bright blue. She wore very long silver earrings; nevertheless her face looked huge — vast, and her voice was hoarse though there was nothing but Vichy water in her glass.

Her small, plump hands were covered with rings, her small, plump feet encased in very high-heeled, patent leather shoes.

Fifi was obvious in fact — no mistaking her mission in life. With her was a young man of about twenty-four. He would have been a handsome young man had he not plastered his face with white powder and worn his hair in a high mass above his forehead.

'She reminds me,' said Mark in a whisper,

'of Max Beerbohm's picture of the naughty lady considering Edward VII's head on a coin — You know, the "Ah! well, he'll always be Tum-Tum to me" one.'

'Yes,' said Roseau, 'she is Edwardian, isn't she?' For some unexplainable reason she disliked these jeers at Fifi, resented them even more than she resented most jeers. After all the lady looked so good-natured, such a good sort, her laugh was so jolly.

She said: 'Haven't you noticed what lots there are down here? Edwardian ladies, I mean — Swarms in Nice, shoals in Monte Carlo! . . . In the Casino the other day I saw . . .'

'Who's the gentleman?' Mark asked, not to be diverted. 'Her son?'

'Her son?' said Roseau, 'Good Heavens, no! That's her gigolo.'

'Her — what did you say?'

'Her gigolo,' explained Roseau coldly. 'Don't you know what a gigolo is? They exist in London, I assure you. She keeps him — he makes love to her, I know all about it because their room's next to mine.'

'Oh!' muttered Mark. He began to sip his aperitif hastily.

'I love your name anyway,' he said, changing the conversation abruptly – 'It suits you.'

'Yes, it suits me – It means a reed,' said Roseau. She had a queer smile – a little sideways smile. Mark wasn't quite sure that he liked it – 'A reed shaken by the wind – That's my motto, that is – Are you going? Yes, I'll come to tea soon – sometime: good-bye!'

'He's running off to tell his wife how right she was about me,' thought Roseau, watching him. 'How rum some English people are! They ask to be shocked and long to be shocked and hope to be shocked, but if you really shock them . . . how shocked they are!'

She finished her aperitif gloomily. She was waiting for an American acquaintance who was calling to take her to lunch. Meanwhile the voices of Fifi and the gigolo grew louder.

'I tell you,' said the gigolo, 'that I must go to Nice this afternoon – It is necessary – I am forced.'

His voice was apologetic but sullen, with a hint of the bully. The male straining at his bonds.

'But, *mon chéri*,' implored Fifi, 'may I not

come with you? We will take tea at the
Negresco afterwards.'

The gigolo was sulkily silent. Obviously the
Negresco with Fifi did not appeal to him.

She gave way at once.

'Marie!' she called, 'serve Monsieur immediately. Monsieur must catch the one-thirty
to Nice. . . . You will return to dinner, my
Pierrot?' she begged huskily.

'I think so, I will see,' answered the gigolo
loftily, following up his victory as all good
generals should — and at that moment Roseau's
American acquaintance entered the restaurant. . . .

They lunched on the terrace of a villa looking
down on the calmly smiling sea. . . .

'That blue, that blue!' sighed Miss Ward,
for such was the American's lady name — 'I
always say that blue's wonderful. It gets right
down into one's soul—don't you think, Mr.
Wheeler?'

Mr. Wheeler turned his horn spectacles
severely on the blue.

'Very fine,' he said briefly.

'I'm sure,' thought Roseau, 'that he's wondering how much it would sell for — bottled.'

She found herself thinking of a snappy advertisement:

'Try Our Bottled Blue for Soul Ills.'

Then pulling herself together she turned to Mr. Leroy, the fourth member of the party — who was rapidly becoming sulky.

Monsieur Leroy was what the French call '*un joli garçon*' — he was even, one might say, a very pretty boy indeed — tall, broad, tanned, clean looking as any Anglo-Saxon. Yet for quite three-quarters of an hour two creatures of the female sex had taken not the faintest notice of him. Monsieur Leroy was puzzled, incredulous. Now he began to be annoyed.

However, he responded instantly to Roseau's effort to include him in the conversation.

'Oh, Madame,' he said, 'I must say that very strong emotion is an excuse for anything — One is mad for the moment.'

'There!' said Roseau in triumph, for the argument had been about whether anything excused the Breaking of Certain Rules.

'That's all nonsense,' said Mr. Wheeler.

'But you excuse a sharp business deal?' persisted Roseau.

'Business,' said Mr. Wheeler, as if speaking

to a slightly idiotic child, 'is quite different,
Miss . . . er . . .'

'You think that,' argued Roseau, 'because
it's your form of emotion.'

Mr. Wheeler gave her up.

'Maurice,' said Miss Ward, who loved peace,
to the young Frenchman, 'fetch the gramophone, there's a good child!'

The gramophone was fetched and the strains
of 'Lady, be Good' floated out towards the blue.

*

The hotel seemed sordid that night to
Roseau, full of gentlemen in caps and loudly
laughing females. There were large lumps of
garlic in the food, the wine was sour. . . . She
felt very tired, bruised, aching, yet dull as if
she had been defeated in some fierce struggle.

'Oh God, I'm going to think, don't let me
think,' she prayed.

For two weeks the Funny One had desperately fought off thoughts. She drank another
glass of wine, looked at Fifi sitting alone at the
mimosa-decorated table with protruding eyes
fixed on the door; then looked away again as
though the sight frightened her. Her dinner
finished she went straight up into her bedroom,

took three cachets of veronal, undressed, lay down with the sheet over her head.

So for about half an hour she lay still as a corpse may be, then suddenly began to sob.

For the Lord had not answered Roseau's prayer. She was thinking.

Suddenly she got up, staggered against the table, said 'Dam,' turned the light on and began to dress, but quietly, quietly. Out through the back door. And why was she dressing anyway? Never mind – done now. And who the hell was that knocking?

It was Fifi. She was wonderfully garbed in a transparent night-gown of a vivid rose colour trimmed with yellow lace. Over this she had hastily thrown a dirty dressing-gown, knotting the sleeves around her neck.

She stared at Roseau, her eyes full of a comic amazement.

'I hope I do not disturb you, Madame,' she said politely. 'But I heard you – *enfin* – I was afraid that you were ill. My room is next door.'

'Is it?' said Roseau faintly. She felt giddy and clutched at the corner of the table.

'You are surely not thinking of going out

now,' Fifi remarked. 'I think it is almost midnight, and you do not look well, Madame.'

She spoke gently, coaxingly, and put her hand on Roseau's arm.

Roseau collapsed on the bed in a passion of tears.

'*Ma petite*,' said Fifi with decision, 'you will be better in bed, believe me. Where is your *chemise de nuit*? Ah!'

She took it from the chair close by, looked rapidly with a calculating eye at the lace on it, then put a firm hand on Roseau's skirt to help her with the process of undressing.

'*Là*,' she said, giving the pillow a pat, 'And here is your pocket handkerchief.'

She was not dismayed, contemptuous or curious. She was comforting.

'To cry is good,' she remarked after a pause. 'But not too much. Can I get anything for you, my little one? Some hot milk with rum in it?'

'No, no,' said Roseau, clutching the flannel sleeve,' 'don't go — don't leave me — lonely —'

She spoke in English, but Fifi responding at once to the appeal answered:

'Pauvre chou — va,' and bent down to kiss her.

174

It seemed to Roseau the kindest, the most understanding kiss she had ever had, and comforted she watched Fifi sitting on the foot of the bed and wrap her flannel dressing-gown more closely round her. Mistily she imagined that she was a child again and that this was a large, protecting person who would sit there till she slept.

The bed creaked violently under the lady's weight.

'Cursed bed,' muttered Fifi. 'Everything in this house is broken, and then the prices they charge! It is shameful. . . .'

'I am very unhappy,' remarked Roseau in French in a small, tired voice. Her swollen eyelids were half shut.

'And do you think I have not seen?' said Fifi earnestly, laying one plump hand on Roseau's knee. 'Do you think I don't know when a women is unhappy? – I – Besides, with you it is easy to see. You look *avec les veux d'une biche* – It's naturally a man who makes you unhappy?'

'Yes,' said Roseau. To Fifi she could tell everything – Fifi was as kind as God.

'Ah! le salaud: Ah! le monstre.' This was said mechanically, without real indignation.

'Men are worth nothing. But why should he make you unhappy? He is perhaps jealous?'

'Oh, no!' said Roseau.

'Then perhaps he is *méchant* — there are men like that — or perhaps he is trying to disembarrass himself of you.'

'That's it,' said Roseau. 'He is trying to — disembarrass himself of me.'

'Ah!' said Fifi wisely. She leant closer. '*Mon enfant*,' said she hoarsely, 'do it first. Put him at the door with a *coup de pied quelque part*.'

'But I haven't got a door,' said Roseau in English, beginning to laugh hysterically. 'No vestige of a door I haven't — no door, no house, no friends, no money, no nothing.'

'*Comment?*' said Fifi suspiciously. She disliked foreign languages being talked in her presence.

'Supposing I do — what then?' Roseau asked her.

'What then?' screamed Fifi. 'You ask what then — you who are pretty — If I were in your place I would not ask "what then," I tell you — I should find a chic type — and quickly!'

176

'Oh!' said Roseau. She was beginning to feel drowsy.

'*Un clou chasse l'autre,*' remarked Fifi, rather gloomily. 'Yes, that is life – one nail drives out the other nail.'

She got up.

'One says that.' Her bulging eyes were melancholy. 'But when one is caught it is not so easy. No, I adore my Pierrot. I adore that child – I would give him my last sou – and how can he love me? I am old, I am ugly. Oh, I know. *Regarde moi ces yeux là!*' She pointed to the caverns under her eyes – '*Et ça!*' She touched her enormous chest. 'Pierrot who only loves slim women. *Que voulez-vous?*'

Fifi's shrug was wonderful!

'I love him – I bear everything – But what a life! – What a life! . . . You, my little one, a little courage – we will try to find you a chic type, a –'

She stopped seeing that Roseau was almost asleep. '*Alors* – I am going – sleep well.'

Next morning Roseau, with a dry tongue, a heavy head, woke to the sound of loud voices in the next room.

Fifi, arguing, grumbling, finally weeping –

the gigolo who had obviously just come in, protesting, becoming surly.

'*Menteur, menteur*, you have been with a woman!'

'I tell you no. You make ideas for yourself.'

Sobs, kisses, a reconciliation.

'Oh Lord! Oh Lord!' said Roseau. She put the friendly sheet over her head thinking: 'I must get out of this place.'

But when an hour afterwards the stout lady knocked and made her appearance she was powdered, smiling and fresh — almost conventional.

'I hope you slept well last night, Madame; I hope you feel better this morning? Can I do anything for you?'

'Yes, sit and talk to me,' said Roseau. 'I'm not getting up this morning.'

'You are right,' Fifi answered. 'That reposes a day in bed.' She sat heavily down and beamed. 'And then you must amuse yourself a little,' she advised. 'Distract yourself. If you wish I will show you all the places where one amuses oneself in Nice.'

But Roseau, who saw the 'chic type' lurking

in Fifi's bulging eyes, changed the conversation. She said she wished she had something to read.

'I will lend you a book,' said Fifi at once. 'I have many books.'

She went to her room and came back with a thin volume.

'Oh, poetry!' said Roseau. She hoped for a good detective story. She did not feel in the mood for French poetry.

'I adore poetry,' said Fifi with sentiment. 'Besides, this is very beautiful. You understand French perfectly? Then listen.'

She began to read:

'Dans le chemin libre de mes années
Je marchais fière et je me suis arrêtée. . . .

. . . .

'Thou hast bound my ankles with silken cords.

. . . .

'Que j'oublie les mots qui ne disent pas mon
     amour,
Les gestes qui ne doivent pas t'enlacer,
Que l'horizon se ferme à ton sourire. . . .

. . . .

'Mais je t'en conjure, ô Sylvius, comme la plus

humble des choses qui ont une place dans ta maison — garde-moi.'

In other words: you won't be rotten — now. Will you, will you? I'll do anything you like, but be kind to me, won't you, won't you?

Not that it didn't sound better in French.

'Now,' read Fifi,

'I can walk lightly for I have laid my life in the hands of my lover.

.   .   .   .

'Chante, chante ma vie, aux mains de mon amant!'

.   .   .   .

And so on, and so on.

Roseau thought that it was horrible to hear this ruin of a woman voicing all her own moods, all her own thoughts. Horrible.

'Sylvius, que feras-tu à travers les jours de cet être que t'abandonne sa faiblesse?
Il peut vivre d'un sourire, mourir d'une parole.
Sylvius, qu'en feras-tu?'

'Have you got any detective stories?' Roseau interrupted suddenly. She felt that she could not bear any more.

Fifi was surprised but obliging. Yes – she had Arsène Lupin, several of Gaston Leroux; also she had 'Shaerlock 'Olmes.'

Roseau chose *Le fantôme de l'Opéra*, and when Fifi had left the room, stared for a long time at the same page:

'Sylvius, qu'en feras-tu?'

Suddenly she started to laugh and she laughed long, and very loudly for Roseau, who had a small voice and the ghost of a laugh.

*

That afternoon Roseau met Sylvius, *alias* the gigolo, in the garden of the hotel.

She had made up her mind to detest him. What excuse for the gigolo? None – none whatever.

There he was with his mistress in Cannes and his mistress in Nice. And Fifi on the rack. Fifi, with groans, producing a *billet de mille* when the gigolo turned the screw. Horrible gigolo!

She scowled at him, carefully thinking out a gibe about the colour of his face powder. But that afternoon his face was unpowdered and reluctantly she was forced to see that the creature was handsome. There was nothing of the blonde beast about the gigolo – he was dark, slim, beautiful as some Latin god. And how soft his eyes were, how sweet his mouth....

Horrible, horrible gigolo! . . .

He did not persist, but looking rather surprised at her snub, went away with a polite murmur: '*Alors, Madame.*' . . .

*

A week later he disappeared.

Fifi in ten days grew ten years older and she came no more to Roseau's room to counsel rum and hot milk instead of veronal. But head up, she faced a hostile and sneering world.

'Have you any news of Monsieur Rivière?' the *patronne* of the hotel would ask with a little cruel female smile.

'Oh, yes, he is very well,' Fifi would answer airily, knowing perfectly well that the *patronne* had already examined her letters carefully. 'His grandmother, alas! is much worse, poor woman.'

For the gigolo had chosen the illness of his grandmother as a pretext for his abrupt departure.

One day Fifi despatched by post a huge

wreath of flowers – it appeared that the gigolo's grandmother had departed this life.

Then silence. No thanks for the flowers.

Fifi's laugh grew louder and hoarser, and she gave up Vichy for Champagne.

She was no longer alone at her table – somehow she could collect men – and as she swam into the room like a big vessel with all sails set, three, four, five would follow in her wake, the party making a horrible noise.

'That dreadful creature!' said Peggy Olsen one night. 'How does she get all those men together?'

Mark laughed and said:

'Take care, she's a pal of Roseau's.'

'Oh! is she?' said Mrs. Olsen. She disliked Roseau and thought the hotel with its *clientèle* of chauffeurs – and worse – beyond what an English gentlewoman should be called upon to put up with.

She was there that night because her husband had insisted on it.

'The girl's lonely – come on, Peggy – don't be such a wet blanket.'

So Peggy had gone, her tongue well sharpened, ready for the fray.

'The dear lady must be very rich,' she remarked. 'She's certainly most hospitable.'

'Oh, she isn't the hostess,' said Roseau, absurdly anxious that her friend's triumph should be obvious. 'The man with the beard is host, I'm sure. He adores Fifi.'

'Extraordinary!' said Mrs. Olsen icily.

Roseau thought: 'You sneering beast, you little sneering beast. Fifi's worth fifty of you!' — but she said nothing, contenting herself with one of those sideway smiles which made people think: 'She's a Funny One.'

The electric light went out.

The thin, alert, fatigued-looking bonne brought candles. That long drab room looked ghostly in the flickering light — one had an oddly definite impression of something sinister and dangerous — all these heavy jowls and dark, close-set eyes, coarse hands, loud, quarrelsome voices. Fifi looked sinister too with her vital hair and ruined throat.

'You know,' Roseau said suddenly, 'you're right. My hotel is a rum place.'

'Rum is a good word,' said Mark Olsen. 'You really oughtn't to stay here.'

'No, I'm going to leave. It's just been sheer

laziness to make the move and my room is rather charming. There's a big mimosa tree just outside the window. But I will leave.'

As the electric light came on again they were discussing the prices of various hotels.

*

But next morning Roseau, lying in bed and staring at the Mimosa tree, faced the thought of how much she would miss Fifi.

It was ridiculous, absurd, but there it was. Just the sound of that hoarse voice always comforted her; gave her the sensation of being protected, strengthened.

'I must be dotty,' said Roseau to herself. 'Of course I would go and like violently some-one like that – I must be dotty. No, I'm such a coward, so dead frightened of life, that I must hang on to somebody – even Fifi –

Dead frightened of life was Roseau, sus-pended over a dark and terrible abyss – the abyss of absolute loss of self-control.

She'd had a bad time, you must know. She was one of those odd people with the instinct of self-preservation entirely lacking. Women first patronized, then disliked her because she was odd – because for some unknown reason

men conceived violent passions for her. Yes,
men desired her, and because she was peculiarly
reckless they usually managed to satisfy their
desire cheaply without much fear of complica-
tions afterwards. What could she do after
all?

Roseau searching, searching for the godlike
face of Love and finding always the grinning
face of Lust – false, shifty-eyed – Roseau getting
up and staggering on, after each blow more
feeble – till the inevitable day when she
wouldn't get up – Done.

There are women like that. Yes. And their
own fault, of course. Listen to all the gentlemen explaining how invariably it is the woman's
fault; listen to the ladies saying: 'Don't tell
me!' So of course I won't.

'Fifi,' said Roseau talking to herself, 'is a pal.
She cheers me up. On the other hand she's a
dreadful-looking old tart, and I oughtn't to go
about with her. It'll be another Good Old
Downward Step if I do.'

Fifi knocked.

She was radiant, bursting with some joyful
tidings.

'Pierrot is returning,' she announced.

'Oh!' said Roseau interested.

'Yes, I go to meet him at Nice this afternoon.'

'I am glad!' said Roseau.

It was impossible not to be glad in that large and beaming presence. Fifi wore a new black frock with lace at the neck and wrists and a new hat, a small one.

'My hat?' she asked anxiously. 'Does it make me ridiculous? Is it too small? Does it make me look old?'

'No,' said Roseau, considering her carefully — 'I like it, but put the little veil down.'

Fifi obeyed.

'Ah, well,' she sighed, 'I was always ugly. When I was small my sister called me the devil's doll. Yes — always the compliments like that are what I get. Now — alas! You are sure I am not ridiculous in that hat?'

'No, no,' Roseau told her. 'You look very nice.'

Dinner that night was a triumph for Fifi — champagne flowed — three bottles of it. An enormous bunch of mimosa and carnations almost hid the table from view. The *patronne* looked sideways, half enviously; the *patron* chuckled, and the gigolo seemed pleased and affable.

Roseau drunk her coffee and smoked a cigarette at the festive table, but refused to accompany them to Nice. They were going to a *boîte de nuit*, 'all that was of the most chic.'

'Ah bah!' said Fifi good-naturedly scornful, 'she is droll the little one. She always wishes to hide in a corner like a little mouse.'

'No one,' thought Roseau, awakened at four in the morning, 'could accuse Fifi of being a little mouse.' Nothing of the mouse about Fifi.

'I'm taking him to Monte Carlo,' the lady announced next morning. She pronounced 'Monte Carl' –'

'Monte Carlo – Why?'

'He wishes to go – Ah! la la – it will cost me something!' She made a little rueful, clucking noise – 'And Pierrot, who always gives such large tips to the waiters – if he knew as I do what *salauds* are the *garçons de café* –'

'Well, enjoy yourself,' Roseau said laughing. 'Have a good time.'

The next morning she left the hotel early

and did not return till dinner-time, late, pre-occupied.

As she began her meal she noticed that some men in the restaurant were jabbering loudly in Italian – but they always jabbered.

The *patron* was not there – the *patronne* looking haughty was talking rapidly to her lingère.

But the *bonne* looked odd, Roseau thought, frightened but bursting with importance. As she reached the kitchen she called in a shrill voice to the cook: 'It is in the *Éclaireur*. Have you seen?'

Roseau finished peeling her apple. Then she called out to the *patronne* – she felt impelled to do it.

'What is it, Madame? Has anything happened?'

The *patronne* hesitated.

'Madame Carly – Madame Fifi – has met with an accident,' she answered briefly.

'An accident? An automobile accident? Oh, I do hope it isn't serious.'

'It's serious enough – *assez grave*,' the *patronne* answered evasively.

Roseau asked no more questions. She took

189

up the *Éclaireur de Nice* lying on the table and looked through it.

She was looking for the 'Fatal Automobile Accident.'

She found the headline:

'YET ANOTHER DRAMA OF JEALOUSY.

'Madame Francine Carly, aged 48, of 7 rue Notre Dame des Pleurs, Marseilles, was fatally stabbed last night at the hotel –, Monte Carlo, by her lover Pierre Rivière, aged 24, of rue Madame Tours. Questioned by the police he declared that he acted in self-defence as his mistress, who was of a very jealous temperament, had attacked him with a knife when told of his approaching marriage, and threatened to blind him. When the proprietor of the hotel, alarmed by the woman's shrieks, entered the room accompanied by two policemen, Mme. Carly was lying unconscious, blood streaming from the wounds in her throat. She was taken to the hospital, where she died without recovering consciousness.

'The murderer has been arrested and taken to the Depôt.'

Roseau stared for a long time at the paper.

'I must leave this hotel,' was her only thought, and she slept soundly that night without fear of ghosts.

A horrible, sordid business. Poor Fifi! Almost she hated herself for feeling so little regret.

But next morning while she was packing she opened the book of poems, slim, much handled, still lying on the table, and searched for the verse Fifi had read:

'Maintenant je puis marcher légère,
J'ai mis toute ma vie aux mains de mon amant.
Chante, chante ma vie aux mains de mon amant.'

Suddenly Roseau began to cry.

'O poor Fifi! O poor Fifi!'

In that disordered room in the midst of her packing she cried bitterly, heartbroken.

Till, in the yellow sunshine that streamed into the room, she imagined that she saw her friend's gay and childlike soul, freed from its gross body, mocking her gently for her sentimental tears.

'Oh well!' said Roseau.

She dried her eyes and went on with her packing.

XXII

VIENNE

Funny how it's slipped away, Vienna. Nothing left but a few snapshots.

Not a friend, not a pretty frock — nothing left of Vienna.

Hot sun, my black frock, a hat with roses, music, lots of music —

The little dancer at the 'Parisien' with a Kirchner girl's legs and a little faun's face.

She was so exquisite that girl that it clutched at one, gave one a pain that anything so lovely could ever grow old, or die, or do ugly things.

A fragile child's body, a fluff of black skirt ending far above the knee. Silver straps over that beautiful back, the wonderful legs in black silk stockings and little satin shoes, short hair, cheeky little face.

She gave me the *songe bleu*. Four, five feet she could jump and come down on that wooden floor without a sound. Her partner, an unattractive individual in badly fitting trousers, could lift her with one hand, throw her in the air — catch her, swing her as one would a flower.

At the end she made an adorable little 'gamine's' grimace.

Ugly humanity, I'd always thought — I saw people differently afterwards — because for once I'd met sheer loveliness with a flame inside, for there was 'it' — the spark, the flame in her dancing.

Pierre (a damn good judge) raved about her. André also, though cautiously, for he was afraid she would be too expensive.

All the French officers coveted her — night after night the place was packed.

Finally she disappeared. Went back to Buda-Pest where afterwards we heard of her.

Married to a barber.

Rum.

Pretty women, lots.

How pretty women here are —

Lovely food.

Poverty gone, the dread of it — going.

ANDRÉ PARISIEN

We soon found a flat — the top floor of General von Marken's house in the Razunoff-skygasse, and André shared it with us for a time.

He was a little man, his legs were too short,

but he took the greatest trouble to have his
suits cut to disguise it.

I mean, with the waist of his coat very high,
almost under the arms, the chest padded,
decided heels to his shoes.

After all these pains what Tilly called his
'silhouette' was not unattractive.

One could tell a Frenchman, Parisian, a
mile off. Quantities of hair which he had waved
every week, rather honest blue eyes, a satyr's
nose and mouth —

That's what André was, a satyr — aged 24.

He'd stiffen all over when he saw a pretty
woman, like those dogs — don't they call them
pointers — do when they see a rabbit — his nose
would go down over his mouth —

It was the oddest thing to watch him at the
'Tabarin' when there was a particularly good
dancer.

He spent hours, all his spare time, I believe,
pursuing, searching.

One day walking in the Kärntnerstrasse we
saw the whole proceeding — the chase, the hat
raising, the snub. He often got snubbed.

He was so utterly without pretence or shame
that he wasn't horrid.

He lived for women; his father had died of women and so would he. *Voilà tout.*

When I arrived in Vienna his friend was a little dancer called Lysyl.

Lysyl and Ossi was her turn – an Apache dance.

She had a wonderfully graceful body, and a brutal peasant's face – and André was torn between a conviction that she wasn't 'chic' enough and a real appreciation of the said grace – He'd lean over the *loge* when she was dancing, breathing, hard eyes popping out of his head –

One night we went with him to some out-of-the-way music-hall to see her, and after her turn was over she came to visit our *loge* – on her best behaviour of course.

I took a sudden fancy to her that night – to her grace and her little child's voice saying:

'Ach, meine blumen – André, André. Ich hab' meine blumen forgessen' – so I snubbed André when he started to apologize – I suppose for contaminating me – and told him – of course he could bring her back to supper.

We squashed up together in one of those Viennese cabs with two horses that go like hell. She sat in a big coat and little hat hugging her *blumen* — in the dark one couldn't see her brute's face.

She really was charming that night.

But next morning, when she came to say good-bye before going, the charm wasn't at all in evidence.

She took half my box of cigarettes, asked by signs how much my dress had cost, ' Why is this woman polite to me,' said her little crafty eyes —

Also most unlucky of all, she met Blanca von Marken on the stairs.

An hour afterwards Madame von Marken had come to see me — to protest.

Blanca was a *jeune fille*. Surely I understood. . . . I would forgive her, but in Vienna they were old-fashioned. . . .

Of course I understood, and against all my sense of fairness and logic apologized and said I agreed.

For God knows, if there's one hypocrisy I loathe more than another, it's the fiction of the 'good' woman and the 'bad' one.

André apologized too, but I'm sure he had no sense of being wanting in logic.

So he grovelled with gusto, feeling chivalrous

as he did so, and a protector of innocence. Oh, Lord!

'Vous savez, mon vieux, je n'ai pas pensé — une jeune fille!'

However, not being Don Quixote I did not even try to protect Lysyl.

I think she could take care of herself.

But though she got on as a dancer and became *mondäne Tänzerin* — I think that's how they spell it — André was done with her.

The fiat had gone forth.

Elle n'a pas de chic.

Because I liked Blanca and Madame von Marken, I even tried to make up for the shock to their virtue by hanging up Franz Josef and all the ancestors — in the sitting-room —

I'd taken them all down in an effort to make the place less gloomy and whiskery and antimacassary — but I saw that it hurt that poor pretty lady — so up they went again and I started living in my bedroom, which was charming.

Very big, polished floor, lots of windows, little low tables to make coffee — some lovely Bohemian glass.

Also I spent much time in the 'Prater.'

VIENNE

Quantities of lilac, mauve and white –
Always now I'll associate lilac with Vienne.

'ANDRÉ' AGAIN

After Lysyl came an interval. André did his
best to fall in love with me –

He thought it against nature to be in such
close touch with a woman (I'd learnt to call him
'Mon vieux copain,' and we said 'Tu' to each
other) without at any rate a few tender passages.

He designed a dress for me, told me that
my hands were a poem.

I said, 'Sad or gay?' He looked blank.

Our conversation was rather full of these
blanks for he did not speak English well, and
my French was even worse than it is now.

Also I was too tall for him – it worried him.
He always used to skip round to the side of the
pavement that slanted upward, but even that was
no good, I still towered, and André gave it up.

We became quite pals at last and he consulted
me solemnly about Ridi's costume.

Ridi was the next arrival, a little girl of perhaps seventeen, eighteen, not more – very shy,
big child's eyes – with fear of the world, of
people, and of pain already there.

She had pretty hands and a graceful little head.

I couldn't have hurt her if I'd been a man, too defenceless, too easy to smash, but few men care a damn about that — or women either.

And at last Tillie — the great, the unique Tillie, the most complete specimen of the adventuress, the Man Eater, I've ever met.

I can't put Tillie at the tail end of a story.

Glory to the Tillies, the avengers of the Ridis!

'TILLIE'

The Radetzsky Hotel was perhaps twenty minutes or half an hour from Vienna by car — and it was real country.

But that is one of the charms of the place — no suburbs.

It wasn't really comfortable; there wasn't a bathroom in the whole establishment, but for some reason it was exciting and gay and they charged enormous prices accordingly.

All the men who made money out of the change came there to spend it, bringing the woman of the moment.

All the pretty people with doubtful husbands

or no husbands, or husbands in jail (lots of men went to jail — I don't wonder. Every day new laws about the exchange and smuggling gold).

Everybody, in fact.

Very vulgar, of course, but all Vienna was vulgar.

Gone the 'Aristokraten.'

They sat at home rather hungry, while their women did the washing.

The ugly ones.

The pretty ones tried to get jobs as *mondäne Tänzerinen*.

Quite right too — perhaps.

Just prejudice to notice podgy hands and thick ankles — keep your eyes glued on the pretty face.

Also prejudice to see stark brutality behind the bows and smiles of the men.

Also prejudice to watch them eat or handle a toothpick.

Stupid too — so much better not to look.

*

The girls were well dressed, not the slightest bit made up — that seemed odd after Paris.

Gorgeous blue sky and green trees and a good orchestra.

201

And heat and heat.

I was cracky with joy of life that summer of 1921.

I'd darling muslin frocks covered with frills and floppy hats – or a little peasant dress and no hat.

*

Well, and Tillie was a queen of this place. It was indirectly through her (she told André) that we got to know of it.

Tillie possessed wonderful eyes, grey-blue – hair which made her look like Gaby Deslys, a graceful figure.

And with that she made one entirely forget a dreadful complexion, four gold teeth, and enormous feet.

This sounds impossible in a place where competition was, to say the least of it, keen, but is strictly true.

Every time one saw Tillie one would think – 'Gee, how pretty she is.' In the midst of all the others everyone would turn to look at her and her gorgeous hair.

And behind walked André, caught at last, held tight 'by the skin,' as the French say.

All his swank was gone – he watched her as

a dog watches his master, and when he spoke
to her his voice was like a little boy's.

She'd flirt outrageously with somebody else
(half the men there had been her lovers so it
was an exciting renewal of old acquaintance-
ships), and André would sit so miserable that
the tears were nearly there.

One night in fact they did come when I
patted him on the arm and said 'Poor old André
– cheer up.'

'Une grue,' said Pierre brutally. 'André is a
fool – And Frances leave that girl alone –'

But I didn't leave her alone at once, too
interested to watch the comedy.

Next Saturday evening we were dining at
Radetzsky with a German acquaintance of
Pierre's.

Excessively good-looking, but, being a
Prussian, brutal, of course.

'*Donner-r-r- wetter-r-r-*' he'd bawl at the
waiters, and the poor men would jump and run.

But perhaps I exaggerated the brutality for
he'd done something I'm still English enough
to loathe – he'd discussed Tillie with great
detail and openness – he'd had a love affair with
her.

Just as we were talking about something else, herself and André hove in sight.

André walked straight to our table and asked if they might join us.

Impossible to refuse without being brutal, though Pierre wasn't cordial, and the other man kissed her hand with a sneer that gave the whole show away.

As for Tillie, she behaved perfectly – not a movement, not the flicker of an eyelash betrayed her – though it must have been trying – just as she was posing as a *mondaine* to meet this enemy openly hostile.

Nor did she let it interfere in the slightest with her little plan for the evening, well thought out, well carried out.

She owned a beautiful pearl necklace which she always wore, and that night she firmly led the conversation in the direction of pearls.

I couldn't do much 'leading,' or indeed much talking in German. I gathered the drift of things, and occasionally Pierre translated.

Tillie's pearls (she told us) were all she had left of a marvellous stock of jewels (*wunderschön*!).

In fact, all she had between herself and destitution, all and all –

Ach – The music chimed in a mournful echo –

She was sad that evening, subdued, eyes almost black, voice sweet and quivery.

After dinner she asked me charmingly if I would mind 'a little walking' – it was so hot – they weren't playing well.

I was quite ready – it was hot – and Tillie went up to her room and came down with a scarf very tightly wrapped round her throat.

We set out. Myself, Pierre and Lieutenant – I've completely forgotten his name – walking together, André and Tillie some little way in front.

Pitch dark in the woods round the hotel – so dark that it frightened me after a while, and I suggested going back.

Shouted to the others, no answer, too far ahead.

We'd got back and were sitting comfortably in the hall drinking liqueurs (alone, for everybody assembled in the bar after dinner to dance) when André came in running – out of breath, agitated.

'The pearls, Tillie's pearls, lost – *Bon Dieu de bon Dieu*. She's dropped them –'

He spoke to me – the only sympathetic listener.

Then entered Tillie. Gone the pathos. She looked ugly and dangerous, with her underlip thrust out.

A torrent of German to Pierre who listened and said in a non-committal way:

'She says that André kissed her in the woods and was rough, and that the clasp of the pearls wasn't sure. It's André's fault, she says, and he'll have to pay up.'

The other man laughed. Suddenly she turned on him like a fury.

'*Mein lieber Herr* . . .' I couldn't understand the words; I did the tone.

'Mind your own business if you know what's good for yourself.'

Meanwhile Pierre, whose instinct is usually to act while other people talk, had gone off and come back with two lanterns and a very sensible proposition.

We would go at once, all four of us, holding hands so that not an inch of the ground should be missed over exactly the same road.

Too dark for anyone else to have picked them up.

Tillie, to my astonishment, didn't seem very keen.

However, we set out in a long row stooping forward. André held one lantern, Pierre the other.

I looked at first perfectly seriously, straining my eyes.

Then André moved his lantern suddenly and I saw Tillie's face. She was smiling, I could swear – she certainly wasn't looking on the ground.

I looked at Pierre – his search was very perfunctory; the other man wasn't even pretending to look.

At that moment I liked André – I felt sorry for him, akin to him.

He and I of the party had both swallowed the story; we were the Fools.

I could have shaken his hand and said:

'Hail, brother Doormat, in a world of Boots.'

But I'd been too sure of the smile to go on looking.

After that I gave all my attention to the little game the German was playing with my hand.

He'd reached my wrist – my arm – I pulled away –

My hand again, but the fingers interlocked.

Very cool and steady his was – and a tiny pulse beating somewhere.

A dispute. We didn't come this way Tillie was saying.

But it had become a farce to everybody but the faithful André.

We went back, but before we'd come within hearing of the music from the hotel, he had comforted her with many promises.

And he kept them too. He turned a deaf ear to all hints that it was or might be a trick.

When we went to Buda-Pest Tillie came. Later on to Berlin, she went too.

She never left him till she could arrange to do so, taking with her every sou he possessed, and a big diamond he'd bought.

This sequel we heard only lately.

Poor André! let us hope he had some compensation for forgetting for once that 'Eat or be eaten' is the inexorable law of life.

The next girl perhaps – will be sweet and gentle. His turn to be eater.

Detestable world.

WAR MATERIAL

'I call them war material,' said Colonel Ishima, giggling.

He meant women, the Viennese women. But when I asked him about the Geisha – I thought it might be amusing to hear about the Geisha first hand as it were – Europeans are so very contradictory about the subject, he pursed up his mouth and looked prim.

'We don't talk about these people – shameful people.'

However, he added after looking suspiciously at a dish of kidneys and asking what they were:

('The innards of the hanimal, sir,' said the waiter tactfully. All the Viennese waiters talk the best Cockney.)

'The Geisha were good people during the war, patriotic people. The Geisha served Nippon well.'

He meant the Russo-Japanese War. One had visions of big blonde Russian officers and slant-eyed girls like exotic dolls stabbing them under the fifth rib, or stealing their papers when they were asleep. . . .

Every fortnight the Japanese officers solemnly entertained their following at Sacher's

Hotel, and they were entertained by ones in return, because in a mass they were really rather overwhelming.

Of course, there it was – the Japanese had to have a following. To begin with, not one of them could speak the three necessary languages, English, German and French, properly. It meant perpetual translation and arguments. And they were dreadfully afraid of not being as tactful as an Asiatic power ought to be, or of voting with the minority instead of the majority, which would have been the end of them at Tokio. . . .

So Ishima had his secretary and confidential adviser (that was Pierre) and Hato had his, and Matsjijiri had his, not to speak of three typists, a Hungarian interpreter and various other hangers-on.

Every fortnight they gave a dinner to the whole lot. It began with caviare and ended with Tokayer and Hato singing love songs, which was the funniest thing I ever heard.

He only had one eye, poor dear; the other disappeared during the Russo-Japanese War. He sang in a high bleat, holding tightly on to one foot and rocking backwards and forwards.

He was very *vieux jeu, arriéré,* a Samourai or something, he wore a kimono whenever he could get into it and he loved making solemn proclamations to the delegation. He called them: *Ordres du jour.*

He made one to the typists, à propos of the temptation of Vienna, which began like this:

'Vous êtes jeunes, vous êtes femmes, vous êtes faibles. Pour l'honneur du Nippon,' etc. etc.

Through some mistake this *ordre du jour* was solemnly brought to an elderly, moustached French general, whilst the Commission was having a meeting to decide some minor detail of the fate of the conquered country. He opened it and read:

'Vous êtes jeunes, vous êtes femmes, vous êtes faibles.'

'M –, alors!' said the general, 'qu'est-ce que c'est que ça' – in his surprise using a famous military expression.

Hato was a great joy. He despised Europeans heartily. They all did that, exception made in favour of Germany – for the Japanese thought a lot of the German Army and the German way of keeping women in their place.

They twigged that at once. Not much they
didn't twig.

But they were all bursting with tact and
Ishima, immediately after his remark about war
material, paid me many flowery compliments.
He hoped, he said, to see me one day in Japan.
The Lord forbid!

After dinner we went to the 'Tabarin.' He
stared haughtily with boot-button eyes at a
very pretty little girl, a girl like a wax doll, who
was strolling aimlessly about, and who smiled
at him very pitifully and entreatingly when she
thought I was not looking.

I knew all about her. She had been Ishima's
friend, his friend acknowledged – *en titre*. She
really was pretty and young. The odd thing
is that the Japanese have such good taste in
European women, whereas European taste in
Japanese women is simply atrocious, or so the
Japanese say.

Well, and Ishima had got rid of her because
she was faithful to him – Odd reason.

It happened like this: He had a visit from a
friend from Japan – a prince of the blood, who
adored plain boiled fish and ate them in a
simple and efficient way, holding them up by

the tail with one hand and using his fork vigorously with the other. Ishima offered him with eastern hospitality everything he possessed — his suite of rooms at the Sacher and the services of his little friend. But the little friend, thinking perhaps to enhance her value, objected — objected with violence, made a scene in fact, and Ishima, more in sorrow than anger, never saw her again.

He just couldn't get over it.

Pierre told me that one day, after meditating for a long time, he asked:

'Was she mad, poor girl, or would others have done the same?'

Pierre answered cautiously that it depended. The ones with temperament would all have made a fuss if only for pride's sake, and the Viennese have nearly as much temperament as the French, the Hungarians even more. On the other hand, the Germans — *Enfin*, it depended.

Ishima meditated a long time. Then he shook his head and said:

'Tiens, tiens, c'est bizarre!' . . .

I thought of the story that night and hated him. He was so exactly like a monkey, and a fattish monkey which made it worse. . . .

VIENNE

On the other hand there was Kashua, who looked even more like a monkey and he was a chic type who had rescued another unfortunate bit of war material deserted without a penny by an Italian officer. Not only did Kashua give her a fabulous sum in yen, but also he paid her expenses at a sanatorium for six months — she was consumptive.

There you are! How can one judge!

Kashua came up grinning and bowing and sat with us. He showed me photographs of his wife — she looked a darling — and of his three daughters. Their names meant: Early Rising, Order, and Morning Sun. And he had bought them each a typewriter as a present.

Then, with tears in his eyes and a quaver of pride in his voice — his little son.

'I think your wife is very pretty,' I told him.

He said, grinning, modestly: 'Not at all, not at all.'

'And I am sure she will be very happy when you will go back to Japan,' I said.

'Very happy, very happy,' he told me. 'Madame Kashua is a most happy woman, a very fortunate woman.'

I said:

'I expect she is.'

Well, Kashua is a chic type, so I expect she is too.

But I believe my dislike of the Viennese nightplaces started at that moment, and I simply jumped at the idea of golf with Fischl as a derivative instead of the 'Tabarin.'

'FISCHL'

WINTER 1920 — SPRING 1921

I met him at the 'Tabarin.'

Simone, Germaine, Pierre, me, a rum Viennese, who wore a monocle and was supposed to live on his very charming wife, two Italians, were dining there.

Fischl arrived to 'kiss the hand,' froze on to me and asked if I'd come to play golf next morning.

The links are near the 'Prater' — and we sat in the nice little house place — drinking hot wine before he started.

It was damn cold for golf.

Also Fischl said my hat was too big and insisted on my taking it off and putting on a sort of mosquito-net thing made of green gauze which covered my face up and fastened at the back.

He wore a white sweater and huge boots.

We sallied out and he started to show me how to hold my club, but all I could think of was how to get at my nose which I wanted to blow.

Also I'd left my handkerchief in the club house.

However, I explained (after two sniffs) to Fischl.

He was quite a sport, undid the mosquito net and lent me his enormous hanky.

Then he said that he was dying to kiss the back of my neck.

It was amusing golf – and we played several times.

He was tall and large with a bushy moustache and a beaky nose, old or oldish.

He talked incessantly of flirting, of London (which he hated), of English people (who amazed him), of himself – of women.

I always remember one long discourse about some place where he'd been in some official capacity.

He talked French, and though my French was improving, there were blanks.

So I only gathered that it was in the Orient.

Turkey, perhaps – or Asia Minor : could it have been Smyrna?

Anyway, there was Fischl. An Important Person.

And every evening he would promenade along the principal street or place or whatever it was and choose a woman.

They sat at windows and passed in carriages.

For all the women were beautiful there – and all were – well, a man had only to choose.

I imagined Fischl walking along, trousers rather tight, moustaches fiercely curling, chest well out. Choosing.

I am not being fair to Fischl, for he was like most Viennese, charming, and clever as hell.

He was fearfully interested in the air raids over London – wanted to know if I remembered the one of such and such a date.

Was there any damage done? And where?

Afterwards I found out that he'd been in Germany during the war and was in some way connected with the air service.

I wonder if he'd anything to do with the bomb that fell so close to the 'Cavour' that night I was with Kinsky?

Golf was too cold for the winter, I decided.

VIENNE

DANCING AT EISENSTEIN'S WITH ANTOINE RENAULT

Horrible man, Eisenstein.

I saw an article in one of the English papers about him.

'The typical Viennese aristocrat,' it said, the dashing cavalry officer who – ruined by the war – is now making his fortune by teaching people to dance, etc. etc. etc.

Yes, I don't think.

Eisenstein is the son of a rich German industrial.

He is an ex-cavalry officer, it is true, but utterly unlike a Viennese aristocrat, and the only dashing thing I ever saw in him was his way of shouting at and bullying his girl assistants.

He does that with a swing and a verve . . . couldn't be better.

Renault – I may say, was the champion breaker of hearts of the French Commission.

He'd caused (they said) several divorces, for he specialized in married women.

He was the sworn enemy of husbands.

He had a special way of saying *le mari* – one felt that to him the poor soul's mission in life was to be made ridiculous (I mean *le mari's*).

He was very attractive in a typically Latin way.

He danced like a – gliding feather – he'd have made a lump dance, he said the most exciting things with a perfectly impassive face and without ever losing step – really exciting and subtly expressed.

But there was always something indefinably wrong about his spats.

If a man ever was born as cleverly sensual as a Frenchman and as attractive as an attractive Englishman, then . . .

Then that man could have any woman he liked.

Luckily, this is extremely rare. The attractive Englishman is a little bit stupid, a little bit 'thick,' more than a little bit an egoist, and a hypocrite.

The Frenchman has metaphorically – something wrong with his spats.

Anyway, Renault fades off with no damage done – to the great relief of Germaine whose property he was.

Simone and Germaine are beginning to look on me with a wary eye.

I can see that they think I'm getting too

uppish for an English girl — whose mission in life is to serve as a foil, with her long teeth and big feet and figure in the wrong place. All French girls think this.

They are first incredulous, then injured, then vindictive, when they meet an Englishwoman who isn't what they think an Englishwoman ought to be.

But they are both too anxious to keep in with Pierre to be anything but very polite, honeyed in fact.

Simone and Germaine are having a *succès fou*.

Simone at least deserves it.

She specializes in English, Americans and French.

Germaine on the other hand has a large following among the Italians, Greeks, and even a stray Armenian who (she says) has offered her fifty thousand francs for one night.

Simone is sublimely conceited.

She told me the other day that Captain La Croix had called her the quintessence of —

French charm, Flemish beauty and Egyptian mystery.

(She was born in Cairo, French mother, Belgian father).

But it is true. She's an attractive little devil.

After Renault, an Italian who explained to me exactly why Vienna is or was 'pure *dix-huitième*.' But he suddenly became amorous.

Scenes by Pierre.

Exit the Italian.

THE LAST ACT OF VIENNA—
THE SPENDING PHASE

I'd noticed people growing more and more deferential to Pierre, and incidentally to me. I'd noticed that he seemed to have money – a good deal – a great deal.

He made it on the change, he told me.

Then one day in the spring of 1921 we left the flat in Razunoffskygasse for rooms in the 'Imperial.'

We sent off the cook and D–, promoted to be my maid, came with us.

Nice to have lots of money – nice, nice.

Goody to have a car, a big chauffeur, rings, and as many frocks as I liked.

Good to have money, money. All the flowers I wanted. All the compliments I wanted. Everything, everything.

Oh, great god money – you make possible all

that's nice in life. Youth and beauty, the envy of women, and the love of men.

Even the luxury of a soul, a character and thoughts of one's own you give, and only you. To look in the glass and think I've got what I wanted.

I gambled when I married and I've won.

As a matter of fact I wasn't so exalted really, but it was exceedingly pleasant.

Spending and spending. And there was always more.

*

One day I had a presentiment.

Pierre gave an extra special lunch to the Japanese officers, Shogun, Hato, Ishima and Co.

We lunched in a separate room, which started my annoyance, for I preferred the restaurant, especially with the Japanese, who depressed me.

It was rather cold and dark and the meal seemed interminable.

Shogun in the intervals of eating enormously told us a long history of an officer in Japan who 'hara-kari'd' because his telephone went wrong during manœuvres.

222

Rotten reason I call it, but Shogun seemed to think him a hero.

Escaped as soon as I could upstairs.

I was like Napoleon's mother, suddenly: 'Provided it lasts.'

And if it does not? Well, thinking that was to feel the authentic 'cold hand clutching my heart.'

And a beastly feeling too — let me tell you.

So damned well I knew that I could never be poor again with courage or dignity.

I did a little sum; translated what we were spending into francs — into pounds — I was appalled — (When we first arrived in Vienna the crown was thirteen to the franc — at that time it was about sixty.)

As soon as I could I attacked Pierre.

First he laughed, then he grew vexed.

Frances, I tell you it's all right. How much am I making? A lot.

How much exactly? Can't say. How? You won't understand.

Don't be frightened, it — brings bad luck. You'll stop my luck.

I shut up. I know so well that presentiments, fears, are unlucky.

'Don't worry,' said Pierre, 'soon I will pull it quite off and we will be rich, rich.'

We dined in a little corner of the restaurant.

At the same table a few days before we came, a Russian girl 24 years of age had shot herself.

With her last money she had a decent meal and then bang! Out –

And I made up my mind that if ever it came to it I should do it too.

Not to be poor again.

No and No and No.

So darned easy to plan that – and always at the last moment – one is afraid. Or cheats oneself with hope.

I can still do this and this. I can still clutch at that or that.

So-and-So will help me.

How you fight, cleverly and well at first, then more wildly – then hysterically.

I can't go down – I won't go down. Help me, help me!

Steady – I must be clever. So-and-So will help.

But So-and-So smiles a worldly smile.

You get nervous. He doesn't understand, I'll make him –

But So-and-So's eyes grow cold. You plead.

Can't you help me, won't you, please ? It's like this and this —

So-and-so becomes uncomfortable; obstinate. No good.

I mustn't cry, I won't cry.

And that time you don't. You manage to keep your head up, a smile on your face.

So-and-So is vastly relieved. So relieved that he offers at once the little help that is a mockery, and the consoling compliment.

In the taxi still you don't cry.

You've thought of someone else.

But at the fifth or sixth disappointment you cry more easily.

After the tenth you give it up — You are broken — No nerves left.

And every second-rate fool can have their cheap little triumph over you — judge you with their little middle-class judgment.

Can't do anything for them. No good.

C'est rien — c'est une femme qui se noie!

But two years, three years afterwards. *Salut* to you, little Russian girl, who had pluck enough and knowledge of the world enough, to finish when your good time was over.

L.B.   225   P

'GELUSTIGE'

She came to the 'Tabarin' with us one night
and I liked her because she spoke such perfect
English and knew in London several people I
had known.

She'd had a house in Mount Street, I think.

Well, Gelustige was a gr-r-r-ande cocotte or
had been.

But she'd had to leave Paris just before the
war —(knew it was coming probably).

She was ugly, fascinating, clever.

She had the wickedest way of smiling or laughing softly to herself. I believe the human comedy
really amused her. She'd reached that stage.

I saw her sizing me up with her wise, cold
eyes.

Two or three nights afterwards, she arrived
to see me.

Pierre and I had quarrelled because again I'd
been insistent on the money question and he'd
gone off to Baden to dine.

I ordered in revenge the most expensive
meal I could choose up to the sitting-room.
She came in the middle of it and sat by the
window drinking Clicquot and getting (for her)
communicative.

What a life that is; what courage it needs.

The constant effort to please, the constant watch over one's nerves.

Never to seem bored, never to seem at a loss.

To learn to accept the most brutal rebuffs with a smile and keep one's dignity.

To learn to guard against other women, to hit them first – quick – before they have time to hit you.

For they will hit – be sure.

And worst of all – the constant effort to keep temperament and senses at top pitch – without – and that is the test – without using drink or drugs to do it.

For when a woman must drink before she can be gay at first and passionate afterwards – then she is no good.

Won't last.

Gelustige, in spite of the war, was fairly comfortable – her friend was a rich Munich banker.

But she regretted Paris.

'Il n'y a que Paris.'

Pierre came in the midst and we finished up at the 'Tabarin.'

She had a wonderful dog, a big curly one.

He kept as close as a shadow to her till we arrived in a restaurant or a night café – then he'd walk straight to the cloak room and lie there with the attendant till we came out.

I've never known a dog trained to the point of that one – he didn't need to be spoken to. He obeyed a nod or a sign.

'INTERMEZZO'

The day before we left Vienna for Buda-Pest was thundery and colder.

I'd spent nearly two hours in a massage place the Russian girl had told me of.

The Russian girl was introduced to me to replace Tillie. She had two advantages: a husband – and a slight knowledge of French.

We'd sat up night after night in the Radetz-sky bar. (Pierre always gathered swarms of people round him.) The most amusing of the party being an old lady of over seventy who wore a bright yellow wig. She'd been an actress and still had heaps of temperament left.

There she sat night after night, drinking punch and singing about Liebe and Frauen with the best.

I came out of the shop and walked down the

strasse — face like a doll's — not a line, not a shadow, eyes nicer than a doll's. Hadn't I had stuff dropped in to make the pupils big and black?

Highly pleased with everything I was that afternoon — with the massage place, with the shortness of my frock, with life in general.

Abruptly the reaction came when I sat down to dinner. I was alone that evening — the presentiment, the black mood, in full swing.

A gentleman with a toothpick gazed fondly at me (in the intervals of serious excavating work), I glued my eyes on my plate.

Oh, abomination of desolation — to sit for two hours being massaged, to stand for hours choosing a dress. All to delight the eyes of the gentleman with the toothpick.

(Who finding me unresponsive has already turned his attention elsewhere.)

I hate him worse than ever.

Franzi is in the hall. The Herr has told him to bring the car and take me for a drive.

Nice Franzi.

I climb in — Go quick, Franzi. Schnell — eine andere platz neit Prater neit weg zum Baden — neit Weiner Wald.

VIENNE

This is my German after two years! I mean go fast. Go to a new place, not the 'Prater,' not the way to Baden —

Yes, that night was the last frenzied effort of my guardian angel, poor creature.

I've never seen so clearly all my faults and failures and utter futility.

I've never had so strong a wish to pack my trunks and clear.

Clear off — Different life, different people.

Work.

Go to England — Be quite different.

Even clearly and coldly the knowledge that I was not being sincere.

That I didn't want to work.

Or wear ugly clothes.

That for ten years I'd lived like that — and that except for a miracle, I couldn't change.

'Don't want to change,' defiantly.

I've compensations.

Oh, yes, compensations — moments.

No one has more.

'Liar, Liar,' shrieked the angel, 'pack your trunks and clear.'

Poor angel — it was hopeless. You hadn't a chance in that lovely night of Vienne.

Especially as in the midst of it came a terrific bump.

In his zeal to find an *andere weg* Franzi had taken me along a road that hadn't been repaired since the year dot. We'd gone right over a stone, so big that I jumped, not being solid, a good three feet into the air. Fell back luckily into the car.

Franzi has stopped and looks behind frightened. I tell him to go home.

It's not my fault.

Men have spoilt me – always disdaining my mind and concentrating on my body.

Women have spoilt me with their senseless cruelties and stupidities.

Can I help it if I've used my only weapon?

Yes, my only one.

Lies everything else – lies –

Lord, how I hate most women here, their false smiles, their ferocious jealousies of each other, their cunning – like animals.

They are animals, probably. Look at all the wise men who think so and have thought so.

Even Jesus Christ was kind but cold and advised having as little as possible to do with them.

Besides, if I went back to London —
I go back to what, to who?
How lonely I am — how lonely I am.
Tears.

Self-pity says the little thing in my brain
coldly is the most ridiculous and futile of
emotions. Go to bed, woman.

I creep in and am comforted. How I adore
nice sheets; how good the pillow smells.

I'm awfully happy really — why did I suddenly get the blues?

To-morrow I'll see Buda-Pest.

Ridiculous idea to go to London. What
should I do in London —

Good-bye Vienna, the lilac, the lights looking
down from Kahlenberg, the old lady with the
yellow wig singing of Frauen.

Will I be ever like the old lady? And run to
the massage shop because I have to prop up the
failing structure? Possibly, probably.

Lovely Vienna. Never see you again.

Nice linen sheets.

Sleep.

Well, we all have our illusions. God knows
it would be difficult to look in the glass without
them.

I, that my life from 17 to 22 is responsible for my damned weakness, and Simone that she has the prettiest legs in Paris.

Good women that they're not really spiteful, bad ones that they're not really growing older or the latest lover growing colder.

'CATASTROPHE'

I can't imagine winter in Buda-Pest. Can't imagine it anything else but hot summer.

Heat and a perpetual smell, an all-pervading smell — in the hotels, in the streets, on the river, even outside the town I still imagined I smelt it.

The Hungarians told us it used to be the cleanest city in Europe till the Bolsheviks made it dirty — the Bolsheviks and 'the cursed, the horrible Roumains.'

It was now being cleaned gradually — very gradually, I should say.

Haughton used to bark loudly (he did bark!) about the exact reasons why it had always been, and still was the most interesting city in Europe, with the exception of Petersburg before the war. 'Les femmes ici ont du chien' — that's how the French officers explained the matter.

Anyway, I liked it – I liked it better than Vienna.

Haughton lived in the same hotel as we did. We took our meals together and every night we made up a party for the Orpheum or one of the dancing places. He generally brought along a bald Italian with kind brown eyes, a sailor, and a Polish woman and her husband.

He was in the Commission because he spoke Russian, German, French, Italian, even a little Hungarian. Marvellous person!

He had lived in Russia for years, tutor or something to one of the Grand Dukes, and I admired his taste in ladies. He liked them slim, frail, graceful, scented, vicious, painted, charming – and he was chic with them from first to last – un-English in fact – though he remained English to look at.

But sometimes he spoilt those perfect nights when we dined outside Buda with his incessant, not very clever cynicisms.

'Ha, ha, ha! Good Lord! Yes. Damn pretty woman. What?'

When the Tziganes were playing their maddest and saddest – he'd still go on happily barking. . . .

234

Buda-Pest looks theatrically lovely from a distance. I remember the moon like a white bird in the afternoon sky; the greyish-green trunks of sycamore trees, the appalling bumps in the road.

'Not too fast, Franzi; don't go too fast!' . . .

Then back to the city and its vivid smells, the wail of Tzigane orchestras, the little dancer of the Orpheum — what was her name? . . . Ilonka — nice name, sounds like a stone thrown into deep water. She would come smiling and silent — she could neither speak French nor German — to sit with us when her turn was over.

'Awfully monotonous this Tzigane stuff — What?' — Haughton would say, fidgeting.

It was, I suppose. It seemed to be endless variations and inversions of a single chord — tuneless, plaintive, melancholy; the wind over the plain, the hungry cry of the human heart and all the rest of it. . . . Well, well. . . .

*

There was a hard, elegant, little sofa in our room, covered with striped, yellow silk — sky-blue cushions. I spent long afternoons lying on that sofa plunged in a placid dream of maternity.

235

I felt a calm sense of power lying in that dark, cool room, as though I could inevitably and certainly draw to myself all I had ever wished for in life – as though I were mysteriously irresistible, a magnet, a *Femme Sacrée*.

One can become absorbed . . . exalted . . . lost as it were, when one is going to have a baby, and one is extremely pleased about it.

*

One afternoon Pierre said: 'If anyone comes here from the Allgemeine Verkehrsbank you must say that I'm not in and that you don't know when I'll be back.'

Someone called from the Bank – a fat, short man, insisting, becoming rude in bad French. He would see Monsieur. He must see Monsieur. Madame could not say when Monsieur would be back. 'Très bien – très bien.' He would go to Monsieur's office to make enquiries.

He departed. His back looked square, revengeful – catastrophic – that's the word. I believe that looking at the man's back I guessed everything, foresaw everything.

I attacked Pierre as soon as he came home. I mean questioned him – but he was so evasive that I turned it into an attack. Evasion has always irritated me.

'Tell me, for Heaven's sake, have you lost a lot of money, or something? You have. I know you have – you must tell me.'

He said: 'My dear, let me alone, I'll pull it off if you let me alone – but I don't want to talk about it. . . . Haughton has asked us to dine at the "Ritz." . . . *Et qu'importent les jours pourvu que les nuits soient belles?*'

He made a large and theatrical gesture.

I let him alone, weakly, I suppose. But one gets used to security and to thinking of one's husband as a money-maker, a juggler, performing incredible and mysterious feats with yen, with lire, with francs and sterling . . . 'change on Zurich. . . .

I let him alone – but I worried. I caught Haughton looking at me as if he were sorry for me. . . . Sorry for me. Haughton!

Ten days after the man of the Bank had called, I went up to my bedroom at half-past six to change my frock and found Pierre sitting on the striped yellow sofa hunched up, staring at the revolver in his hand.

I always hated revolvers, little, vicious, black

things. Just to look at a revolver or a gun
gives me a pain deep down in my head – not
because they're dangerous – I don't hate knives
– but because the noise of a shot hurts my ears.

I said: 'Oh, Pierre, put that thing away!
How horribly unkind you are to frighten
me!'

Stupid to cry at the very moment one should
keep calm!

He was silent, rather surly.

Well, I dragged the truth out of him. He
told me, moving one foot restlessly and looking
rather like a schoolboy, that he had lost money –
other people's money – the Commission's
money – Ishima had let him down. . . .

Then followed the complicated history of
yens – of francs – of kronen. He interrupted
himself to say: 'You don't understand a thing
about money. What is the good of asking me
to explain? I'm done, I tell you, tried everything . . . no good! I may be arrested any time
now.'

I was calm, cool, overflowing with common
sense. I believe people who are badly wounded
must be like that before the wound begins to
hurt. . . . Now then, what is the best way to

stop this bleeding? . . . Bandages. . . . Impossible that this and no other is the shot that is going to finish one. . . .

I sat on the sofa beside him and said: 'Tell me how much you need to put yourself straight? I can understand that much at any rate.'

He told me, and there was a dead silence.

'Leave me alone,' he said. 'Let me put a bullet in my head. You think I want to go to jail in Buda-Pest? I haven't a chance!'

I explained still calmly and reasonably that he must not kill himself and leave me alone — that I was frightened — that I did not want to die — that somehow I would find the money to pay his debts.

All the time I was speaking he kept his eyes on the door as if he were watching for it to open suddenly and brutally. Then repeated as if I had not spoken: 'I'm fichu. . . . Go away and let me get out of it the only way I can. . . . I've saved four thousand francs ready money for you. . . . And your rings. . . . Haughton will help you. . . . I'm fichu. . . .'

I set my mouth: 'You aren't. Why can't you be a man and fight?'

'I won't wait here to be arrested,' he

answered me sulkily, 'they shan't get me, they shan't get me, I tell you.'

My plan of going to London to borrow money was already complete in my head. One thinks quickly sometimes.

'Don't let's wait then. Pierre, you can't do such a rotten thing as to leave me alone?'

'*Mon petit*,' he said, 'I'm a damn coward or I would have finished it before. I tell you I'm right – I'm done. Save yourself. . . . You can't save me!'

He laughed with tears in his eyes. 'My poor Francine, wait a bit. . . .'

'Let's go, let's get away,' I said, 'and shut up about killing yourself. If you kill yourself you know what will happen to me?'

We stared at each other.

'You know damn well,' I told him.

He dropped his eyes and muttered: 'All right – all right! . . . Only don't forget I've warned you, I've told you. It's going to be hell. . . . You're going to blame me one day for not getting out quick and leaving you to save yourself.'

He began to walk restlessly up and down the room.

We decided that we would leave early the next morning. Just to go off. Like that. We made plans — suddenly we were speaking in whispers. . . .

We had dinner upstairs that night, I remember — *paprika, canard sauvage* — two bottles of Pommery.

'*Allons,* Francine, cheer up! *Au mauvais jeu il faut faire bonne mine.*'

I've always loved him for these sudden, complete changes of mood. No Englishman could change so suddenly — so completely. I put out my hand, and as I touched him my courage, my calm, my insensibility left me and I felt a sort of vague and bewildered fright. Horrible to feel that henceforth and for ever one would live with the huge machine of law, order, respectability against one. Horrible to be certain that one was not strong enough to fight it.

'Au mauvais jeu bonne mine.' . . . A good poker face, don't they call it? . . . The quality of not getting rattled when anything goes wrong. . . .

When we opened our second bottle of Pommery I had become comfortingly convinced that I was predestined – a feather on the sea of fate and all the rest. And what was the use of worrying – anyway? . . .

As I was drinking a fourth glass, hoping to increase this comforting feeling of irresponsibility, Haughton knocked and came in to see us.

There was a moment that night when I nearly confided in Haughton.

Pierre had gone away to telephone, to see the chauffeur, and I've always liked those big men with rather hard blue eyes. I trust them instinctively – and probably wrongly. I opened my mouth to say: 'Haughton, this and that is the matter. . . . I'm frightened to death, really. . . . What am I to do?' . . .

And as I was hesitating Pierre came back.

*

At one o'clock we began to pack, making as little noise as possible. We decided to take only one trunk.

I remember the table covered with cigarette-ends and liqueur-glasses, the two empty bottles of champagne, and the little yellow sofa looking rather astonished and disapproving.

'THE FLIGHT'

At half-past six in the morning we left the hotel.

That journey to Prague was like a dream. Not a nightmare; running away can be exhilarating but endless as are certain dreams, and unreal.

While I dressed and finished packing my hands had trembled with fright and cold, but before we left Buda-Pest behind us the hunted feeling had vanished.

There is no doubt that running away on a fresh, blue morning can be exhilarating.

I patted the quivering side of the car, gazed at Franzi's stolid back, wondered if he guessed anything, and decided he probably did, sung 'Mit Ihrem roten Chapeau.' After all, when one is leaving respectability behind one may as well do it with an air.

The country stretched flatly into an infinite and melancholy distance, but it looked to me sunlit and full of promise, like the setting of a fairy tale.

About noon we passed through a little plage on the Danube; it must have been Balaton, and there were groups of men and girls walking about in short bathing-suits. Nice their brown

legs and arms looked and the hair of the girls
in the fierce sun.

Pierre called out: 'Hungry?'

I said: 'Yes.'

But I grew uneasy again when we stopped
for lunch at some little village of which I was
never to know the unpronounceable name.

Through the open door of the restaurant
the village looked bleak in the sunlight and
pervaded with melancholy; flocks of geese,
countless proud geese, strolled about; several
old women sat on a long, low stone bench under
a lime tree, on another bench two or three old
men. The old women were really alarming.
Their brown, austere faces looked as though
they were carved out of some hard wood, the
wrinkles cut deep. They wore the voluminous
dark skirts, handkerchiefs tied round their
heads, and they sat quite silent, nearly motion-
less. How pitiless they would be those ancient
ones to a sinner of their own sex – say a thief –
how fiercely they would punish her. Brrrrr!
Let us not think of these things.

Pierre said: 'What a life they must have,
these people!'

I agreed: 'Dreadful!' looked away from the

stone bench, drank my horrible coffee, and went outside. There was a girl, a maid of the inn perhaps, or a goose-girl, going in and out of the back door, carrying pails and tubs. She wore a white bodice so thin that one could plainly see the shape of her breasts, a dark skirt, her feet were bare, her head was small, set on a very long neck, her eyes slanted like Ishima's – I watched her with an extraordinary pleasure because she was so slim and young and finely drawn. And because I imagined that when she glanced at me her eyes had the expression of some proud, wild thing – say a young lioness – instead of the usual stupid antagonism of one female looking at another.

I said to Pierre: 'Oh, I do think that Hungarians can be lovely; they beat the Austrians hollow.'

He answered so indifferently: 'Another type,' that I began to argue:

'The Austrians are always trotting out their rotten old charm that everybody talks about. Hate people who do that. And they're fat and female and *rusé* and all the rest.'

'Oh!' said Pierre, 'and if you think that Hungarians aren't *rusé*, my dear, *zut*! – they are the most *rusé* of the lot, except the Poles.'

I insisted: 'In a different way. . . . Now look at that girl; isn't she lovely, lovely?'

'*Un beau corps*,' judged Pierre. 'Come on, Francine, let's get off if you are ready.'

I heard the apprehension in his voice and climbed into the car a little wearily. A grind . . . and we had left behind us that goose-girl out of a fairy tale against her background of blue distances quivering with heat.

I began to plan my triumphant return to Hungary with money to pay Pierre's debts. I saw myself sitting at the head of a long table handing little packets of notes to everyone concerned, with the stern countenance of a born business-woman: 'Will you sign this, please?'

Then I must have slept, and when I woke I'd begun to feel as if the flight had lasted for days, as though I could not remember a time when I hadn't been sitting slightly cramped, a little sick, watching the country fly past and feeling the wind in my face.

Pierre turned and asked if I were tired or cold.

'No, I'm all right. . . . Are you going to drive? Well, don't go too fast . . . don't break our necks after all this.'

246

We left the flat country behind and there was a sheer drop one side of the road. The darkness crept up, the wind was cold. Now I was perfectly sure that it was all a dream and could wait calmly for the moment of waking.

We flitted silently like ghosts between two rows of dark trees. I strained my eyes to see into the frightening mystery of the woods at night, then slept again and the car had stopped when I woke.

'What is it?'

'The frontier . . . keep still. . . .'

An unexpected fuss at the frontier. There was a post. A number of men with rifles round a wood fire, an argument which became very loud and guttural. Our passports were produced:

'Kommission – Kurrier.'

'What is it, Pierre?'

He got out of the car without answering and followed one of the men into the shelter.

It was horrible waiting there in the night for what seemed hours, my eyes shut, wondering what jail would be like.

Then Pierre re-appeared, still arguing, and got in beside me.

247

He muttered: 'Je m'en fiche, mon vieux,' and yelled to the chauffeur.

The car jumped forward like a spurred horse. I imagined for one thrilling moment that we would be fired on, and the nape of my neck curled itself up. But when I looked back over my shoulder I saw the knot of men by the light of the fire looking after us as if they were puzzled.

'Frightened?'

'No, only of being sent back. What was it? Had they been told to stop us?'

'No, but nobody is supposed to pass. The frontier is shut, something has happened.'

I said: 'What can it be, I wonder,' without the slightest interest.

'Well,' said Pierre, 'here is Czechoslovakia, and good-bye Hungary!'

'Good-bye, Hungary!' Tears were in my eyes because I felt so tired, so deathly sick.

*

'You're awfully tired, aren't you, Frances?'

'A bit. I'd like to rest. Let's stop soon. Where will we spend the night?'

'At Presburg. We're nearly there.'

I huddled into a corner of the car and shut my eyes.

It was late when we found a room in the
Jewish quarter of the town. All the good hotels
were full; and in the hardest, narrowest bed I
had ever imagined I lay down and was instantly
asleep.

Next morning something of the exhilaration
had come back. We went out to breakfast and to
buy maps. It had been decided that we would
go to Prague and there sell the car, and then . . .

'I want to go to Warsaw,' announced Pierre.

I said dismayed: 'Warsaw? but, my dear . . .'

The coffee was good, the rolls fresh; something in the air of the clean, German-looking
little town had given me back my self-confidence.

I began to argue: 'We must go to London
. . . in London . . .'

'*Mon petit,*' said Pierre, lighting his pipe, 'I
don't believe in your friends helping us. I
know how naïve you are. Wait, and you will
see what your famous friends are worth. You
will be *roulée* from the beginning to the end.
Let's go to Warsaw. I believe I can arrange
something there; Francine, do what I say for
once.'

I told him obstinately that I did not like
Poles. He shrugged his shoulders.

249

We found the car and Franzi waiting at the hotel.

'Off we are,' said Pierre, cheerfully, '*en route*! Here's the brandy flask.'

The road was vastly better, but I had no comforting sensation of speed, of showing a clean pair of heels. Now we seemed to be crawling, slowly and painfully, ant-like, across a flat, grey and menacing country. I pictured that dreary flatness stretching on and on for miles to the north of Russia, and shivered.

I kept repeating to myself: 'I won't go and be buried in Poland. . . . I won't go. . . . I don't care. . . . I will not. . . .'

The wind was cold; it began to drizzle persistently.

'Pierre, we're off the road, I'm sure. That woman put us wrong. This is only a cattle-track.'

It was. And time was wasted going backwards. Pierre cursed violently all the while. He had begun to be in a fever of anxiety to reach Prague. . . .

*

The walls of the bedroom where we slept that night were covered with lurid pictures of

Austrian soldiers dragging hapless Czecho-
slovakians into captivity. In the restaurant
downstairs a pretty girl, wearing a black
cape lined with vivid purple, sat talking to
two loutish youths. She smoked cigarette
after cigarette with pretty movements of her
hands and arms and watched us with bright
blue, curious eyes.

We drank a still wine, sweetish, at dinner. It
went to my head and again I could tell myself
that my existence was a dream. After all it
mattered very little where we went. Warsaw,
London. . . . London, Warsaw. . . . Words!
Quite without the tremendous significance I
had given them.

It was still raining when we reached Prague
at last. We made the dreary round of the
hotels; they were all full, there were beds in the
bathrooms of the hotel du Passage; it was an
hour before we discovered a room in a small
hotel in a dark, narrow street.

Pierre began to discuss the sudden return of
King Karl to Hungary. We heard the news at
the Passage.

That was the trouble at the frontier, of
course.

I said indifferently – I was lying down – 'Yes, probably.'

Karl – the Empress Zita – the Allies – Commission – the Whites – the Reds –Pierre himself . . . shadows! marionnettes gesticulating on a badly lit stage, distracting me from the only reality in life . . . the terrible weight that bowed me down . . . the sickness that turned me cold and mounted up to cloud my brain.

Pierre advised me to have some strong coffee. He rang the bell and a short, fat waiter appeared who looked at me with that peculiar mixture of insolence, disdain, brutality and sentimentality only to be found amongst those of German extraction.

Then he departed to fetch the coffee.

It was an odd place, that hotel, full of stone passages and things. I lay vaguely wondering why Prague reminded me of witches. . . . I read a book when I was a kid – *The Witch of Prague*. No. It reminded me of witches anyhow. Something dark, secret and grim.

'I think Prague is a rum place,' I told Pierre. 'What's that bell that keeps ringing next door?'

'A cabaret, cinema perhaps. . . . Listen, Frances, it's just the best of luck for us, that business of Karl. Nobody will worry about me just now. Ishima will be far too busy voting with the majority. . . . *Sacré* little Japanese!'

'Probably,' I agreed.

He asked me if I felt ill, suggested a doctor.

'A Czech doctor, my God!'

I pulled the sheets over my head. I only wanted to be left alone, I told him.

'Francine,' said he gently, 'don't be a little silly girl. The doctors are good here if you want one.'

He put the rug over me: 'Rest a bit while I go and see about the car. We'll dine at the "Passage" and find a dancing afterwards. Yes?'

I emerged from under the sheets to smile because his voice sounded so wistful, poor Pierre.

About six that evening I felt suddenly better and began to dress.

Because I noticed at lunch that the grand chic at Prague seemed to be to wear dead black I groped in the trunk for something similar, powdered carefully, rouged my mouth, painted a beauty spot under my left eye.

I was looking at the result when Pierre came in.

'My pretty Francine, wait a bit! I have something here to make you chic . . . but chic . . .'

He felt into his pocket, took out a long case, handed it to me.

'Pierre!'

'Nice, *hé*?'

'Where did you get them?'

He did not answer.

I looked from the pearls to his dark, amused face, and then I blushed — blushed terribly all over my face and neck. I shut the case and gave it back to him and said: 'How much money have we got left?' And he answered without looking at me: 'Not much; the worst is this war-scare. Czechoslovakia is going to mobilize. It won't be so easy to sell the car. We must sell it before we can move. Never mind, Francine.'

I said: 'Never mind!' Then I took the case, opened it, clasped the pearls round my neck. 'If we're going the whole hog, let's go it. Come on.'

One has reactions, of course.

Difficult to go the whole hog, to leave respectability behind with an air, when one

lies awake at four o'clock in the morning –
thinking.

'Francine, don't cry . . . what is it?'

'Nothing. . . . Oh! do let me alone. . . .'

When he tried to comfort me I turned
away. He had suddenly become a dark stranger
who was dragging me over the edge of a
precipice. . . .

It rained during the whole of the next week,
and I spent most of the time in the hotel bedroom staring at the wallpaper. Towards evening I always felt better and would start to
think with extraordinary lucidity of our future
life in London or Paris – of unfortunate
speculation and pearls – of a poker face and
the affair of King Karl. . . .

*

One day of the end of our second week in
Prague Pierre arrived with two tickets which
he threw on the bed: 'There you are, to Liège,
to London. . . . I sold it and did not get much;
I tell you.' . . .

I spent an hour dressing for dinner that
night. And it was a gay dinner.

'Isn't the *chef d'orchestre* like a penguin?'

'Yes, ask him to play the Saltimbanques Valse.'

255

'That old valse?'

'Well, I like it . . . ask him. . . . Listen, Pierre, have we still got the car?'

'Till to-morrow.'

'Well, go to the garage and get it. I'd like to drive like hell to-night. . . . Wouldn't you?'

He shrugged: 'Why not?'

Once more and for the last time we were flying between two lines of dark trees, tops dancing madly in the high wind.

'Faster! Faster! Make the damn thing go!'

We were doing a hundred.

I thought: he understands — began to choose the tree we would smash against and to scream with laughter at the old hag Fate because I was going to give her the slip.

'Get on! . . . get on! . . .'

We slowed up.

We were back at the hotel.

'You're drunk, Frances,' said Pierre severely.

I got out, stumbled, laughed stupidly — said: 'Good-bye! Poor old car,' gathered up the last remnants of my dignity to walk into the hotel. . . .

It was: 'Nach London!'